Beecher Island

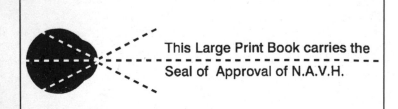

This Large Print Book carries the
Seal of Approval of N.A.V.H.

BEECHER ISLAND

A WESTERN STORY

TIM CHAMPLIN

THORNDIKE PRESS
A part of Gale, Cengage Learning

Detroit • New York • San Francisco • New Haven, Conn • Waterville, Maine • London

GALE
CENGAGE Learning

Copyright © 2010 by Tim Champlin.
Thorndike Press, a part of Gale, Cengage Learning.

Thorndike Press® Large Print Western.
The text of this Large Print edition is unabridged.
Other aspects of the book may vary from the original edition.
Set in 16 pt. Plantin.

LIBRARY OF CONGRESS CATALOGING-IN-PUBLICATION DATA

Champlin, Tim, 1937–
    Beecher Island : a western story / by Tim Champlin.
        p. cm. — (Thorndike Press large print western)
    ISBN-13: 978-1-4104-2954-4
    ISBN-10: 1-4104-2954-7
    1. Large type books. I. Title. II. Series.
PS3553.H265B44 2010b
813'.54—dc22   2010037049

Published in 2010 by arrangement with Golden West Literary Agency.

Printed in the United States of America
1 2 3 4 5 6 7 14 13 12 11 10

For my granddaughter,
Alice Rose Champlin
Health and Happiness, Always!

PART ONE

CHAPTER ONE

August, 1868
Camp of Cheyenne Chief, Bull Bear
Solomon River, western Kansas

"Why you come?" Bull Bear asked as he used a callused thumb to pack tobacco into the bowl of a long pipe.

It wasn't like the wizened old Cheyenne to skip over the traditional courteous amenities, Matt Talbot thought, as he, Abner "Sharp" Grover, and fellow scout, Bill Comstock, sat cross-legged on blankets in the chief's teepee. Perhaps the old Indian was nervous about the throng of insolent young bucks milling around outside. All three white men knew they were safe only as long as they were guests of Bull Bear.

"The trail to your last camp shows many riders joined you," Grover replied in the Cheyenne tongue in deference to his old friend. Matt knew the experienced Grover didn't want to question directly — at least

9

until they'd smoked as a sign of friendship.

"Yes. Young men come to our band." The chief paused to press a coal from the fire to the pipe bowl and puff it to life. Then he passed it across the tiny cooking fire. Grover held the pipe solemnly to each of the cardinal points of the compass, taking a puff at each direction like a priest incensing four altars. He passed the pipe to Comstock who repeated the process, the pungent tobacco smoke blending with the wood smoke to drift upward toward the open flap in the top of the conical tent. Matt was the last to smoke, copying the ceremony the older men had just performed. He handed the pipe back to Bull Bear, who sat impassively, apparently waiting for Grover to continue.

"We are here to speak for the bluecoat chief, Lieutenant Beecher," Grover said. "He sent us to ask you to lead your people back south to the reservation."

Bull Bear took another puff of the pipe, then set it down beside him. His eyes, bright and alert behind sagging folds of skin, regarded Grover through curls of smoke. His copper face was a map of fine lines and wrinkles, framed by white hair drawn tightly and tied at the back of his neck. A lone eagle feather hung down from his scalp lock. The feather was dyed red, showing its wearer had been wounded, and the edges were serrated, indicating at least four coups. This old chief had earned his place of leadership. "I carry the weight of many winters," he finally replied. "I am tired. I wish to live in peace on the reservation. But these young men would stay and hunt in the land of our fathers."

"Your young men are not just hunting buffalo," Grover replied in English, since Bull Bear had a working knowledge of the language, while Comstock and Talbot understood only a few words of Cheyenne. "They also raid wagons and kill white ranchers who do no harm to your people. They shot the railroad workers."

Talbot knew Grover wasn't sure, but was gambling this band of Cheyennes had taken part in depredations earlier in the summer.

"Your people steal land," Bull Bear replied in English. "Your iron horse cuts buffalo hunting grounds." He demonstrated a cutting motion with the edge of his hand. "Scare game. Indians come to land to hunt. Whites come to stay."

Grover stared down at his stained leather leggings, without replying immediately.

Talbot, at twenty-four, the youngest and least experienced negotiator of the three, watched and listened. What could Grover say to that? The old chief spoke the truth. In his aboriginal mind, this theft of land justified any raiding and killing.

Grover tried another tack. "It was written at Medicine Lodge that the Cheyennes, Comanches, Arapahoes, Osages, Pawnees, and Kiowas would stay on reservations, leaving them only for buffalo hunting."

Talbot had read the treaty signed at Medicine Lodge, Kansas the previous October. Even for someone as literate as he, it was a complicated document, and Grover had simplified it rather well. It involved a white peace commission of several hundred soldiers headed by General Sherman, along with an appointed group of civilians sympathetic to the Indians. Tons of supplies were distributed to the tribes. Representatives of the plains tribes who made their mark on the treaty document were promised food, clothing, housing, and vocational training programs if they stayed on the reservations south of Kansas in the Indian Territory.

"I was not at Medicine Lodge," the old man replied, "but I traveled south to live on reservation. My band stayed there until the Moon of New Grass, but white chiefs gave us no meat, no blankets."

Congress had taken the better part of a year to ratify the treaty; only now had the promised provisions begun to trickle in to the tribes in the Indian Territory.

"It took much time for these things to happen," Grover said, apparently unable to justify the delay.

"My people starve. We had to hunt," Bull Bear said.

And kill in retaliation, Talbot thought.

"If I start tomorrow for reservation, take jerked meat and hides we gather, only a few old men and women follow me. I cannot force young men to go. They will stay and fight."

"They cannot win," Grover said. "The white soldiers are as many as the grains of sand on the riverbed." A wild exaggeration, and Bull Bear probably knew it. But Talbot thought it a good visual image. In the years during and since the war, the chief had likely seen with his own eyes only a few scattered patrols of the bluecoats. Not more than a few dozen manned the forts dotting the Kansas trails. How could Grover convince this Indian the government could muster many thousands of soldiers?

"Your warriors will die if they fight," Grover continued. "The mighty Cheyenne people will be no more." He ripped a handful of dry bunch grass from the ground beside his blanket and dropped it onto the cooking fire. The grass curled up as the flame consumed it. Where neither man was fluent in the other's language, blatant imagery was best understood, Talbot thought. "Were these young men who joined your band from Roman Nose?"

At the mention of the great Cheyenne leader, Bull Bear looked sharply at Grover. "You know much, my friend. Yes, they are Cheyennes, like our people. Roman Nose is coming south again. He brings many warriors and new rifles. The Arapahoes and Sioux come with him."

Although it was hot in the closed teepee, Talbot felt a chill run up his sweaty back at this. Was Bull Bear only bragging? Most tribes were too independent to band together against the whites. Indian pride and old animosities rarely permitted such a thing. But he went cold at the thought of Roman Nose leading a coalition of Sioux and Arapahoes, some of the fiercest fighters and best horsemen on the plains.

Grover seemed unfazed and didn't even ask where the new rifles might have come from.

"Roman Nose has been in many battles," Bull Bear went on. "He has strong medicine. White man's bullets not touch him."

"Good medicine can turn bad like meat

14

that rots," Grover said.

"We will see," the old chief countered.

He's played his ace, Talbot thought. Grover and Bull Bear had known each other for a dozen years, but their personal trust and respect couldn't bridge the chasm between their cultures. This discussion was going nowhere. Neither of them had any real power to alter events, and Talbot sensed both of them realized it.

"That's all we can do here," Comstock said quietly with a shrug. "Let's ride." He seemed a bit fidgety at the murmuring of voices just outside the teepee. It resembled the sound of swarming bees. If Grover was nervous, he didn't show it.

"You must leave this place," Bull Bear said. "I will see you safely out of camp. Then I can no longer protect you."

Grover unfolded his legs and climbed stiffly to his feet.

The old chief slid the blanket from his shoulders, rose, and threw back the hide tent flap. He pointed to several of those outside and said something in Cheyenne. Bull Bear turned to Grover. "Some of my young men will ride south with you until the sun sets."

Grover nodded to the chief and ducked outside. The three whites retrieved their horses and mounted up. "Keep your hands away from your guns," Grover muttered to Comstock and Talbot. The chief scout had a Colt in his holster and a Henry rifle in the saddle scabbard. Comstock and Talbot both carried .36-caliber 1862 model Colts. Sullen young braves, mounted bareback on ponies, pressed close about them, repeating rifles in their hands.

Two warriors rode on each side and one led the way as they started at a trot. The sun on their right was nearing the flat, western horizon. No one spoke.

Talbot was relieved to be riding out and felt relatively safe in the presence of this escort, handpicked by Grover's friend, Bull Bear. But he heard the soft rumble of other hoofs and turned in his saddle. Six or seven young Indians were trailing them sixty yards to the rear, maintaining a steady distance behind.

By the time they'd covered another mile, the sun sank from sight and the beginning of a long twilight began spreading across the treeless landscape.

At a brief word from the rider in front, the escort of five veered away and left the three white scouts. Grover reined up and watched them gallop away back toward their camp. When the escort had gone two hundred yards, the trailing Indians came on at a gallop.

"Let's run for it, Sharp!" Comstock urged.

"Too late," Grover replied. "Hold still and see what they want."

The Indians rode up on both sides and Talbot needed no interpreter to get the gist of their jeering remarks. "Ignore them," Grover said, quietly, touching his horse with his heels. The animal started ahead at a walk, followed by Comstock and Talbot. A minute later the three urged their mounts to a trot.

The young braves kept pace. Two of them had Sharps carbines, and the others were armed with bows and full quivers. The Indians shouted what appeared to be insults at the two men. Talbot knew Grover understood what they said, but he kept silent, trotting straight ahead.

Dusk was stealing over the prairie. Maybe these young bucks were just having a little fun and showing off for each other. Except for one, they looked too young to have seen any real warfare. Finally Grover nudged his horse alongside Comstock. "Crow Feather," he said, nodding toward the oldest looking of the group. "From Roman Nose's band."

"Let's go," Comstock replied, kicking his mount into a gallop.

The Indians kept up for a quarter mile, but gradually began dropping back.

Thank God, we're going to get out of this without a fight, Talbot thought.

Then a shot blasted from behind and Talbot saw Grover reel in the saddle. The plainsman yanked the Henry rifle from its scabbard, cocked, and swung around to fire the rifle with one hand.

Two more shots sounded from the darkness and suddenly Comstock's saddle was empty. "Bill!" Grover yelled.

Talbot leaned over his horse's neck and began firing wildly behind them with his revolver. As he looked up, Grover slumped over the saddle horn just as Comstock's riderless horse bumped his. Grover pitched forward out of the saddle.

Indians were yelling to each other and several thundered past Talbot, circling the two fallen riders. Talbot leaped off his mount, still holding the reins, but the startled animal jerked the reins from his hand and plunged away.

Unhurt, Talbot threw himself on the ground, pistol in hand, hoping they wouldn't see him in the dark, or would think him dead. A minute later, he saw the silhouettes of the Indians against the lighter sky as they rounded up all three horses, leading them away. *After our damned horses and gear,* he thought. *Bastards thought no more of shooting us than prairie chickens!*

He waited until their hoof beats faded into the distance, then jumped up and holstered his pistol. "Sharp! Bill! Where are you?" He strained to see his fallen comrades. His stomach tensed. *God, were they both dead?* "Grover! Comstock! Can you hear me?" His voice was low, urgent. No answer. He had a premonition of disaster. They had to be close by.

At last he saw a dark lump on the ground. There were no rocks on this grassy prairie; it had to be something else. He sprang toward it and crouched beside Bill Comstock. No pulse. From what he could tell in the dark, a large caliber slug had caught him squarely in the upper back. "Damned cowards!" he hissed through gritted teeth, wiping his sticky hand on the scout's shirt. "I can't believe they did this!" He stood up. "Grover!" He stumbled around in a circle, feeling with his feet for what he couldn't see and feared to find.

"Here!" Grover's husky voice called a few yards away.

"You hit?"

"Yeah. Got me in the back of the shoulder." He struggled to his feet, one arm

19

hanging down. "Where's Bill?"

"Over there. Dead."

Grover staggered to Comstock's still form and sank to his knees. "Gawd, Bill. Never thought it'd end like this." He took several deep breaths. "Reckon we'll have to let the coyotes and buzzards have your carcass. But you ain't really here, are you? So you'll never know."

He pulled Comstock's pistol from its holster and shoved it under his belt. Then he placed his hand on his friend's tangled hair in silent farewell. As Talbot watched from a respectful distance, Grover rocked back on his haunches and pushed erect.

"If this ain't a helluva note," Grover said. "We took a big chance riding into Bull Bear's camp."

"The old man did what he could to protect us," Talbot said.

"Shore did. Warn't his fault. Those young hotheads in his band don't have no respect for anything. It's always the young ones ready to fight. Kill a man for his horse or gun. Reckon it's the way they're taught. Have to live as long as Bull Bear to get any sense." He moved toward Talbot, gripping his upper arm with one hand. "Me and Bill Comstock go back a long way. Now he's shot in the back . . . for nothing." His voice broke, and he paused, breathing heavily. Talbot was glad he couldn't see this hardened frontiersman's show of emotion. Grover took several long breaths. "Time to go," he finally said. "See if you can help me out of this jacket and bind up this wound until it stops bleeding."

Talbot eased the man's buckskin jacket off and used his knife to cut the one clean sleeve off the older man's shirt to use for a bandage. The bullet had struck the upper arm muscle from behind and the slug was still imbedded. He passed the cotton shirt sleeve under the arm and over the shoulder, tying it tight. "That's as good as we can do for now."

"Thanks, Matt. Find my Henry on the ground over there, will ya?"

After a couple minutes of searching, Talbot located the rifle.

"Reckon we're afoot," Grover said, taking the Henry. "You still got some powder and shot?"

"Always keep a supply in my jacket," Talbot said. "Just in case."

"Good. Hope you don't need it, but it's a long walk back to the fort."

"I'll carry your jacket until you need it," Talbot said. He wondered how far away the fort was, but hesitated to ask. It'd seemed like many miles when they rode out here on horseback. He was thirsty, and could only imagine the thirst Grover must feel, having lost a good amount of blood. But the horses were gone with their canteens.

Grover paused and looked up at the spangled heavens. "Well, there's the North Star, so we'll head off south." He started walking and Talbot fell in beside him.

The two of them, on foot, with no food or water, isolated miles from any white settlement — a daunting prospect, Talbot thought. But Grover seemed to take things as they came and not complain or voice any fear. Undoubtedly he'd encountered and survived similar situations.

They walked in silence for several minutes. Then Grover said: "If we keep up a steady pace, we'll likely intersect the Kansas-Pacific railroad by daylight."

Talbot immediately felt better. The empty prairie didn't seem as vast. And he was young and strong and not wounded.

But it proved to be a very long night, interrupted by frequent stops. A partial moon rose and looked down on their lonely trek. Twice Grover thought he saw a form moving in the distant moonlight. "Reckon I'm seeing things," he muttered. "Ain't likely some lone warrior is trailing us. They already got what they wanted." He paused and rubbed his eyes. "I did see *something*. Probably a hunting wolf off yonder. Too far away to tell in the moonlight."

"Wolf won't bother us," Talbot said.

"Naw. A lone wolf won't come near two men. If it were winter and there was a hungry pack of 'em, then we'd have to be careful. But in high summer, there's plenty of small game around." He chuckled. "Glad you're here, though. Iffen I was to pass out from loss of blood, some critter might come along and start gnawing on my carcass."

"Yeah." Sometimes Grover's sense of humor was a little rough.

Slowly Talbot's thirst increased. "You familiar with this part of the country?" he asked, to take his mind off his dry mouth and throat.

"Sort of," Grover replied. "Cricks and small rivers in this part of Kansas drain from west to east by north. They sort of parallel each other, but they're miles apart."

Talbot tried to picture a map in his mind. Before he could form a good mental image, Grover stopped and said: "Lookee yonder."

"What?"

"Down in that swale . . . see the dark line of trees? A sure sign of water in this country."

■ ■ ■ ■

An hour later, they were kneeling on a sandy bar, scooping up cool, sweet water in cupped hands. Nothing had ever tasted so good, Talbot thought. They rested for a quarter hour and Talbot unbound Grover's stiffened arm and bathed the wound, washing his bloody shirt while he was at it.

The moon was on the wane when they set out again, feeling refreshed. Talbot carried the loaded Henry, which seemed to gain weight with every mile. They trudged on silently in the darkness after moonset, mile after weary mile. Talbot's mind was in a fog.

Dawn crept up over the plains before he was even aware of it. They stopped for a breather and hunkered down to rest the muscles in their backs and legs. Grover pointed. Far off to the southwest, Talbot could just make out a small herd of antelope grazing. He rubbed his tired eyes, then stood up. They pressed on.

The sun rose, slanting its rays across the gently rolling grassland. As the air warmed, a light morning breeze sprang up, bringing scents of fresh earth and growing things.

Grover paused and stared off to the south. "I'll likely leave my bones out here someday, like the buffalo and all the other critters," he muttered aloud. "I just hope it ain't today."

Abner Grover had been nicknamed "Sharp" by his friends because of his hawk-like eyesight and powers of observation. Two hours later, as they topped a slight rise, he stopped and pointed. "Look there." Even Talbot's eyes could pick out a thread-thin gleam in the distance, bisecting their path. "The Kansas-Pacific rails."

The railroad disappeared as they continued walking toward it the rest of the morning. Just before noon, they finally crept up the graded right of way. Grover knelt and put his ear to one of the iron rails. "Don't hear nothing. *Uh* . . . my legs are about give out."

"How's the arm?"

"Feverish. Think I'll lie down here in the sunshine and take a little rest."

"Sounds like a good idea."

The two men stretched out on the grassy slope.

Talbot tipped his hat over his face. After walking all night, this grass felt heavenly. That was his last thought before he fell asleep.

The ground trembled, startling him awake.

His eyes flew open and he instinctively rolled away from the track, staggering stiffly to his feet on the slope. Sweating and thirsty, heart pounding from sudden exertion, he snatched off his hat and flagged the oncoming work train.

Brakes screeching, the slow-moving, dark blue mogul locomotive ground to a stop ten yards away, blasting jets of steam from either side. A trainman swung down from the cab and ran forward. Talbot and Grover came up to meet him.

"What happened to you two?" the fireman asked, looking them up and down.

"You bound east to Fort Hays?" Grover asked. "We need a ride."

CHAPTER TWO

"Come in and close the door, Mister Grover," Colonel John Weatherly said, waving Sharp and Matt Talbot to a wooden bench against the wall.

Three other men were already in the room.

"Damn, I hope this meeting is short," Grover whispered to Talbot as they sat down. "I gotta get this arm tended to." He adjusted the makeshift sling.

They'd arrived at Fort Hayes only an hour earlier and been shown into the base commander's office where they briefed Colonel Weatherly.

The colonel stood behind his desk and gestured toward the uniformed men in the room. "Mister Grover, Matthew Talbot, I believe you know Lieutenant Fred Beecher, Colonel George Forsyth, and Sergeant Jacob McCall."

Grover nodded to the three men. "Let's

get on with this," he gritted to Talbot under his breath. "I'm feeling rough."

Talbot averted his eyes from raw-boned Sergeant Jake McCall, who was glaring at him. McCall's hawk-like nose was bent at an angle, the result of a barroom fight three months earlier. Talbot knew the details of that skirmish since he was the one who'd given a very drunk and belligerent McCall the right cross that crooked his nose.

"I've related your story to these men," the colonel was saying. "And let me say we're all very sorry for the loss of your friend, Bill Comstock."

"We never had a chance," Grover said. "Bull Bear did what he could, but a bunch of renegades followed and shot us from behind."

Weatherly nodded. "His death will not go unavenged." He picked up a sheet of paper from his desk. "Let me read you a telegraph message I received this morning. It concerns all of you." He slipped on his reading spectacles. "Headquarters, Department of the Missouri . . . and so forth." He skipped ahead. "This is addressed to Brevet Colonel George A. Forsyth. Colonel . . . the general commanding directs that you, without delay, employ fifty first-class hardy frontiersmen, to be used as scouts against the hostile

Indians, to be commanded by yourself, with Lieutenant Beecher, Third Infantry, your subordinate. You can enter into such articles of agreement with these men as will compel obedience." He looked up. "It's signed by the Adjutant for General Phil Sheridan."

Weatherly laid the paper on the desk. "Well, Sandy," he said, addressing Colonel Forsyth, "the general didn't waste any time granting your request for command in the field."

"More than one way to skin a cat," Forsyth said with a smile.

Talbot knew Forsyth only to see him around the Kansas forts. He was a career officer, a handsome thirty-year-old who wore his thick hair somewhat shorter than that of the other officers, and sported only a sweeping trooper's mustache in place of the more stylish goatee or side whiskers. He'd seen a lot of action in the Civil War and had a reputation for courage and intelligence.

"Scouts instead of soldiers," Lieutenant Beecher said. "A great idea, sir. And these will be men of experience. Not raw recruits."

"Mister Grover," the colonel said, coming around the desk to stand in front of him, "Colonel Forsyth would like you to be chief of these scouts. How about it?"

"I'm agreeable, as long as Lieutenant

Beecher is second in command," Grover said. "Of course, you realize most of these scouts are going to be older than your average soldier. Some of them served in the military during the war and had a bellyful of taking orders. You're gonna have a more independent bunch on your hands than you might expect."

Talbot glanced toward the bullying Sergeant Jake McCall, hoping he'd gotten the message.

"I'll take experience over subservience every time," Lieutenant Beecher said.

"These men won't be undisciplined, sir," Sergeant McCall spoke up. "I'll see to it."

Talbot looked up. McCall had served as an officer in the Union forces during the war, and only recently come back into the depleted military as an enlisted man. Talbot thought he was probably pushing to get his commission back.

"There are enough frontiersmen around these forts to easily recruit fifty good men," Weatherly said. "Start here, and then go east to Fort Harker. The general said the Army somehow found enough money to pay seventy-five dollars per month if each man supplies his own horse, and fifty dollars if the Army furnishes a mount. That should entice some good men who'd welcome some quick cash and promise of a little excitement."

"I recognized Crow Feather among those renegades who gunned us down," Grover said.

Weatherly frowned. "Doesn't he run in the band led by Roman Nose?"

"Yup. A bunch o' them are joining forces with the Arapahoes and Sioux."

"Not a good sign. But maybe your column of scouts can disrupt all that before they combine in force. Harass them, keep them on the run. At least give them something to think about so they won't have time to raid ranches and kill settlers."

"Colonel, the cold weather might drive 'em to the reservations in a couple months," Talbot spoke up.

"Not likely, if they harvest enough buffalo to see them through the winter. Besides, we can't wait that long. The Kansas governor has written to President Johnson, demanding action."

Grover wiped his sweating face, even though Talbot thought the room was comfortable with a breeze blowing in through the open window.

"That's all, gentlemen," Colonel Weatherly said, and they rose to leave. The colonel stepped over to Grover and put a hand on his forehead. "Man, you're burning up with fever. Get on over to the post hospital and let Doctor Mooers have a look at that wound."

"Yes, sir."

CHAPTER THREE

Fort Harker, Kansas
Eighty miles east of Fort Hays

Matt Talbot leaned on the counter of the sutler's store and inhaled the mingled aromas of coffee, tobacco, and new leather. He scanned the shelves, trying to recall what he needed. At least three bandannas, a notebook, and pencils. . . .

"Can I help ya, mister?"

A clerk moved into his vision.

"Yeah, let me see your largest bandannas." Talbot shifted his gaze to the young man behind the counter. "Phil Granger! What're you doing in this neck o' the woods?" Talbot burst out. "Last I heard you were making big money working for the Kansas-Pacific at end of track."

"Matt Talbot!" The taller man seemed taken aback. "Damn!" He thrust out his hand and the two shook. "Didn't reckon I'd run into you at Fort Harker."

Talbot lowered his voice, looking for the sutler, who was in the back room. "None o' my business, but you're cut out for better things than this."

"This is just a short stop for me to get a grubstake," Granger said under his breath. "Got a good selection of bandannas over here," he continued aloud, reaching up to a shelf. "Injuns jumped our work crew . . . twice in less than a week," he said. "Cheyennes and Arapahoes. Killed three men. Division superintendent shut down the operation for a spell. Laid everybody off. Don't know for how long."

Talbot flashed a grin. "It's a mighty ill wind that doesn't blow somebody good," he said. "Since the Army has cut back, there aren't enough troops to protect the railroad builders and settlers. Some general up the line has said the Army could hire a troop of fifty civilian scouts to go hunting for these renegade bands of Indians who won't go to the reservations. I signed up."

"Thought you had your fill of fighting in the war," Granger said.

"*Aw,* hell, this scout won't be like that. We'll get paid and fed for riding around the country tracking those bands. You can bet they'll stay clear of us. Like as not, the only thing we'll see of Indians is pony turds and tracks."

"You really think so?" Granger arched his brows.

"Damn' right. Those renegades like to strike quick and hard at any defenseless targets. They kill a few, run off some horses, try to force the whites into leaving this part of the country. But when it comes to fighting any pitched battles with armed scouts or soldiers . . . that's another stink in the breeze altogether. This'll be a lark for you after that heavy work on the railroad." He glanced toward the door to the storeroom, but saw the boss wasn't within earshot. "Come along and sign up. Colonel Forsyth is still trying to round up enough men. I recollect you being a good rider. You got a horse?"

Granger nodded. "A good one."

"They're paying seventy-five dollars a month if you got your own mount," Talbot continued. "I'd bet that's a good bit more than your wages here. And the military will furnish everything we need."

"I'm tempted. But I'm a few years older than you, and I need to get into some kind of career," Granger mused. "I want a skill I can fall back on. Can't afford to be wasting much more time. I'd like to get married and settle down before I'm an old man."

"I know what you mean. During the winters when there ain't much doing, I been trying to teach myself to set type," Talbot said. "I want to be a printer someday. Only a few of these forts have newspapers, but I go off to these little towns and take whatever job they got, even work for grub, just to get experience and learn the trade."

Selecting several bandannas, Talbot then asked about notebooks and pencils. Granger then stuffed the bandannas, notebook, and pencils into a paper sack and took the coins Talbot handed over.

"Come and sign up," Talbot reverted to his former suggestion, with urgency. "It'll be like old times. You and I got some catching up to do. This job won't last more than a month or two at most. And it'll be a lot more fun than what you're doing now, I'll wager. It'll be an adventure."

Granger ran a hand through his thick, blond hair and pursed his lips.

"Better decide right away before Colonel Forsyth gets enough men," Talbot said. "He's here now, but he's moving on tonight."

"OK," Granger decided suddenly. "Let me collect my pay and I'll meet you out front in a few minutes."

■ ■ ■ ■

Two days later at Fort Hays, a burly man wearing a sergeant's stripes faced twenty men in the quartermaster's storeroom. "I'm Sergeant McCall. You're here to draw your equipment. Every man will sign for it, or make his mark. You'll return all this in good order, or your pay will be docked. Line up here."

A rough-looking group, several bearded and in buckskins, shuffled forward along the counter, each accepting one Spencer repeating carbine with one hundred and forty rounds of .56-caliber ammunition; a Colt Army revolver with thirty rounds of paper cartridges in a leather cartridge box; one blanket; a butcher knife; tin plate and cup; canteen and haversack; lariat and picket pin; and, lastly, a bridle and hornless McClellan military saddle.

A corporal manned a small table at the end of the line with a ledger book and each man set his load on the floor before taking the quill to affix his signature. Talbot noticed the calloused fingers awkwardly scrawling names or personal marks that were witnessed by the soldier. These were hands more adept with axes, rifle, or reins. Talbot signed his name with a flourish, and gathered up his load. He staggered out into the sunshine to meet Granger who'd already drawn his gear. He'd leave his own saddle and most of his few articles of clothing here at Fort Hays until the column returned.

On the afternoon of August 29th, Major George Forsyth and Lieutenant Fred Beecher led the rag-tag column out of Fort Hays. Laughing and talking, the men were in high spirits and seemed eager for the chase. The group of horsemen numbered fifty-five. Talbot was feeling lazy on this warm, late summer day as he rode, stirrup to stirrup, beside Phillip Granger, near the rear of the column. He thanked whatever providence controlled his fate that he was in the saddle again with a fresh west wind bending his hat brim. Life was good.

"Doubt if this bunch would strike terror into any renegade Indian band," Talbot remarked, inclining his head at the bending, straggling column ahead of them. They were as odd an assortment of men as he'd ever seen in one place — farmers in blue and brown denim, laborers in red flannel shirts, several horsemen in cast-off cavalry breeches with reinforcing leather sewn inside the legs. Talbot noted vests, fringed buckskin jackets, boots, and leggings. A variety of wide-brimmed hats topped long hair and shaded bearded faces. Teamsters, laborers, farmers, adventurers, former buffalo hunters, and guides had signed on. Just a jumble of faces, but he'd get to know them before this was through.

"Spit and polish never impressed any Injun I ever saw," Granger said. "But you're right about the one thing useful to this outfit, the Spencers and the Colts we're all carrying."

"Hell, I feel like a neophyte," Talbot said.

"Talk English," Granger said.

"Tenderfoot."

"Not hardly. There's a kid here some place who's all of seventeen. Smallish lad. Looks about thirteen . . . Sigmund Schlesinger. He was a messenger between the forts. Sold newspapers and magazines. But I'm told he can stick like a horsefly to the back of a mount, and he wanted to tag along in the worst way, so Lieutenant Beecher finally gave in and let him come."

"I'd guess a goodly number of these men are veterans, like me."

Granger nodded. "That's right."

In the time they'd known each other, Talbot seldom talked about the war. He'd seen a minimum of fighting, working mostly as a courier between a headquarters company and officers in the field during the latter days of the war in Tennessee when he was only nineteen. Although he had been brought to America by his widowed mother when he was only five years old, to escape the Great Hunger, he retained little of his Irish brogue.

"I heard a bunch of men last night calling themselves Solomon Avengers," Granger said. "What was that all about? Thought we were to be known as Forsyth's Scouts."

"Bunch of sodbusters," Talbot replied. "Indians raided and burned their homesteads along the Solomon River."

They rode all afternoon, and plodded on when the sun dropped behind a cloudbank just before sunset. Two hours later, a drizzling rain set in. The officers didn't call a halt until 11:00 that night when they made a fireless camp along the Saline River.

It rained steadily all the next day, making for a dreary, uncomfortable ride. There was no banter among the scouts. They rode, hunched over, covered with ponchos and slickers, water dripping from bent hat brims. In spite of all he could do, Talbot's pants and saddle got damp and his skin began to chafe.

Lieutenant Beecher and half a dozen men fanned out in advance to serve as guides for the rest, and to give themselves a better chance of cutting Indian sign.

"Hell, they're serious about all this, aren't they?" Granger said when the column halted and dismounted, to rest and let the horses and pack mules forage on the prairie grass.

Just then one of the advance scouts, a man named Joe Lane, came galloping in, reined up, and blurted out he'd seen Indians several miles ahead. Major Forsyth took his field glasses and rode up the long slope to take a look, while the troop nervously awaited the outcome. He returned, saying it was a herd of grazing antelope.

Shortly after, the command went into camp on the south fork of the Solomon River.

The next day, September 1st, dawned bright and sunny. The column reached Beaver Creek, traveling upstream for fifteen miles without seeing any sign of the elusive Indian bands.

He never mentioned how sore he'd been, but Talbot felt an inner satisfaction that he was beginning to harden from this routine of riding and camping. They rode up a slight rise out of the alluvial valley of Beaver Creek. The gently undulating land rolled like billows on an endless ocean.

Talbot pulled out of the column and reined up. "Look." He pointed into the distance. The early afternoon sun was striking the tops of clouds boiling thousands of feet into a blue sky. The whiteness of it hurt his eyes. Beneath this awesome display, eighty some miles away, lay an anvil of solid black storm clouds. Between that and the earth, gray veils of rain swept the plains. Now and then a stab of lightning winked, but no sound reached them from the far-away storm.

"Like watching the Almighty pull a curtain across half the world," Talbot said quietly, removing his hat and feeling the gentle breeze drying the sweat under his long brown hair.

"Sure ain't nothin' gonna sneak up on us out here," the practical Granger said, glancing around at the wide-open landscape. "Unlessen they come up out of one o' these swales."

Talbot watched the display for a full minute, breathing deeply of the fresh air before rejoining the column. He pulled in behind the string of pack mules that carried their extra provisions and ammunition. No one was conversing. The sounds of the column's movement were quickly swallowed up by an eternal stillness — the soft thudding of hoofs, leather squeaking, the clank and rattle of a canteen against a buckle or carbine barrel.

An hour later they topped a rise and saw thousands of buffalo grazing in a loose herd several miles ahead. The column altered course to pass behind the drifting herd.

In late afternoon, the scouts came upon an abandoned Indian camp. Some of the experienced men said it looked two weeks old.

While the column waited for orders, Barney Day, a small, lean scout, rose from examining the dead ashes of a campfire and swung up into his saddle. He turned to Forsyth. "Major, what little sign we've seen so far shows these bands went north and west after they raided in the Saline and Solomon River valleys . . . I'd guess they headed up yonder toward the Arikaree River region."

The major nodded, looking frustrated. He turned to Lieutenant Beecher. "We'll swing south, and start back for Fort Wallace to re-outfit."

The word was passed to Sergeant McCall, and the column moved out.

■ ■ ■ ■

At mid-morning, September 5th, Major Forsyth galloped back from the point, and yelled something to the lieutenant. Beecher wheeled his horse and shouted at Sergeant McCall. A wave of excitement swept back along the column as McCall came riding past, shouting: "Indians ahead! Prepare to attack!"

Heart pounding, Talbot pulled his carbine from the loop on his saddle.

"Damn! Injuns right near the fort!" Granger yelled across at him.

"Charge!" Sergeant McCall bellowed.

Talbot kicked his mount to a gallop, following after the troop thundering over a gentle rise, dust boiling from hundreds of hoofs, obscuring what lay ahead.

Gunfire rattled and shouts rose on the air. In less than a minute, the column veered left.

"Hold! Hold! Cease fire!" Lieutenant Beecher's voice was barely audible over the rumble of hoofs and exploding shots.

Talbot bumped the rider in front of him and nearly dropped his Spencer as he tried to control his wildly plunging horse. From the corner of his eye he saw a scout flung from his saddle and disappear in the tangle of horses' legs.

Talbot managed to clear the mêlée and rein up, walking his trembling, excited horse. He shoved his carbine back into its loop, then reached for his Colt. "Phil! What the hell happened?" he shouted.

Granger, several yards away, didn't answer.

Finally a sweating, red-faced Sergeant McCall rode back through the milling riders. "False alarm! False alarm! Just a bunch of haymakers from the fort."

A breeze was shredding the dust cloud to reveal three men on the ground, lifting the scout who'd been thrown from his horse. In the distance, Major Forsyth conferred with several white men, some of whom were still afoot.

Will Bennet, the scout who'd been thrown from his horse and kicked, had to be carried in a makeshift litter between two horses the rest of the afternoon as the column slowly rode toward Fort Wallace. The men spoke in subdued voices and more than one glanced at the blue uniformed figure of Major George Forsyth at the head of the column. Embarrassment and resentment hung as heavily in the air as the irritating dust.

Granger and Talbot, by choice, rode near the rear of the column just in front of the pack mules. The horses plodded on into the dusk and darkness, pushing toward Fort Wallace. Near midnight, the weary, hungry column rode into the parade ground and began dismounting.

Talbot loosened the cinch strap on his mount. "That wouldn't have happened if Sharp Grover had been with us," he said under his breath in the darkness, finally voicing his disgust. "Hope to hell that wound is well enough for him to leave the hospital and join us."

"Well, I'm not one to talk about lack of experience," Granger said. "But, then, I'm not in command here."

"Forsyth was a colonel in the war, so he must've been a good soldier, but he can't tell prairie chicken feathers from eagle feathers when it comes to Indians," Talbot said, grunting as he tugged off his saddle. Earmarks of disaster were beginning to appear on this scouting "picnic."

CHAPTER FOUR

The command rested four days at Fort Wallace, and the scouts took full advantage of the break to catch up on sleep and food. Three men dropped out due to illness and Will Bennett, the man thrown from his horse in the mistaken attack, was admitted to the post hospital with a simple leg fracture and a concussion. Sharp Grover's wound was healed sufficiently for him to rejoin the column.

Although he admitted it only to Granger, Talbot was grateful for a few days to recover from his soreness after too many hours in the saddle. Maybe he wasn't cut out for a job that required this many continuous hours on horseback. A good thing he wanted eventually to be a printer, learn the skills of a typesetter and the rest of the printing business, so he'd never lack for a job. Writing for a paper or magazine was a secondary aspiration, fueled by a natural inclination and love for literature. To this end, keeping a daily journal would be good practice.

"You about ready to ride?" Granger asked, leading his horse out of the stable into the bright sunshine of the parade ground where the other scouts were milling around.

"Just about," Talbot replied, stuffing his saddlebags with strips of jerky from the sutler's. His new journal and writing utensils were wrapped in an extra pair of socks. He didn't use tobacco, so that was one thing he didn't have to stock. He rolled up his rain slicker and secured it with leather saddle ties.

He glanced out at the flag fluttering on the pole in the middle of the sunny, hard-pack parade ground. "One thing about this being a civilian outfit," he said to Granger, "is that we don't have to start at dawn or earlier like the soldiers always seem to do. Somebody ought to tell those officers there are other times of day besides five in the morning."

He buckled the saddlebags and hooked them over the brass stud behind the seat of the McClellan saddle.

"I notice the major reads books," Granger observed.

"All officers do, I expect."

"Maybe. But, novels?"

"Really? On the march?"

"Saw Major Forsyth with a copy of Dickens's *Oliver Twist*."

"Since he's not supposed to fraternize, I guess it beats sitting around the campfire listening to the crickets chirp."

There was a general stirring of horses and men while the troop prepared to depart.

The door to the commandant's office banged shut as Lieutenant Fred Beecher came out onto the porch, and raised his arm. "Men! Let me have your attention!" he shouted above the hubbub. A few looked his way. "Be quiet for a minute!"

The scouts shuffled toward him, leading their horses.

Beecher held up a paper. "Received a telegraph message from Sheridan, Kansas, thirteen miles east. An Indian war party just attacked a freighting caravan there. Killed two teamsters and ran off some livestock."

Major George Forsyth came out the door, drawing on his gauntlets, and stood beside his lieutenant on the porch. "Sergeant Mc-Call, mount the column. We're riding to Sheridan."

In just under an hour the scouts arrived at the scene of the attack. Two Mexican teamsters who were shot had also been scalped.

"War party's long gone," Granger said quietly as he dismounted. Forsyth, afoot, examined the two bodies while he listened to the story from a big, bearded man.

"Twenty or twenty-five of them," the man said in a booming voice. He nodded toward the two bodies. "They'd fallen behind for just a couple of minutes when those damned redskins picked them off. Run off a few mules, too." He paused and shot a stream of tobacco juice into the dry grass. "Sure wish you boys or the Army or somebody would do sumpin' about them renegades. Ain't no place safe in Kansas any more."

Forsyth muttered something Talbot couldn't hear, then swung into the saddle. "Let's ride, men. This is the first solid trail we've had. Let's make the most of it while we got plenty of daylight."

The trail was easy to follow since the two dozen unshod ponies and half dozen mules had chopped up the grass and moist loam of the prairie sod. Talbot was no tracker, but the obvious trail led straight away toward the northwest.

The column rode the rest of the day without catching sight of the fleeing war party. At nightfall Forsyth ordered a dry camp when they halted.

By daylight they were in the saddle again,

alternately trotting and walking the horses.

"Don't know how I can get so stiff in only one day," Talbot complained to Granger as they rode side-by-side.

"We covered a lot of miles yesterday," the bigger man replied. "And the major was pushing pretty hard."

Today, the two men had chosen to ride near the front of the column to avoid most of the dust being churned up by the animals' hoofs. Thus, they were close enough to hear Major Forsyth when he called a halt at mid-morning to confer with his subordinates.

Sharp Grover, Lieutenant Beecher, and two other riders had been scouting the terrain a hundred yards in advance and either side of the column. They rode in and sat their horses in a circle around Forsyth.

"They're up to their old tricks, Major," Grover said. "One or two at a time are dropping off from the main group. They aim to meet up somewhere far ahead after they've thrown us off the track."

"And it appears they're splitting away where the ground is hard or brushy, so individual trails are harder to follow," Lieutenant Beecher added, grimacing as he shifted in the saddle, apparently to ease the pain of the old Civil War knee wound. Talbot saw why the man was so admired.

51

Instead of a hard life in the cavalry, Fred Beecher could have used his New England connections to obtain a comfortable job in civilian life. Not only was he youthful and handsome, but he was also the nephew of author Harriet Beecher Stowe and her brother, the famous preacher, Henry Ward Beecher.

"The trail is still leading north," Grover said. "I reckon those Indians plan on meeting up again at their main encampment somewhere in the Arikaree River country."

No one spoke for several seconds.

"By the time we locate 'em, they'll have a combined force of tribes a lot bigger than we'll be able to handle, Major," Grover said. "You think it's wise to keep after 'em?"

"We came to find and attack these Indians, no matter what the odds," Major Forsyth snapped. "We'll continue north for as long as it takes."

Talbot wondered if this dogged determination reflected the major's dispassionate devotion to following orders, or if there might be a burning vengeance behind the words.

For the next several days, the column continued to ride north, even after all sign of a trail had disappeared. The experienced scouts and trackers were convinced they knew approximately where the large encampment would be.

On the morning of September 14th, one of the outriding scouts stumbled across the remains of an abandoned brush wickiup concealed among the stunted willows along a stream. They followed the dim trail leading away from the shelter. Within a few miles they came upon an abandoned campsite Grover and the other plainsmen affirmed was less than twenty-four hours old.

Sergeant McCall ordered the scouts and mule packers to speak only in low voices, and to secure their equipment and loads to avoid any rattling of gear.

The month of September had turned dry, with large, unproductive thunderheads building in the distance every afternoon. The sun and prevailing west wind had sucked all the moisture out of the soil and the yellowing prairie grass, allowing the animals to churn up clouds of dust.

"Major, that dust cloud we're raising can be seen for miles," Sergeant McCall said. "We're proclaiming our coming like the pillar of cloud that went before the Israelites in the desert."

"Or the pillar of fire that led them by night," Forsyth added, as if talking to himself. He twisted in his saddle to squint at the rising dust. "Spread out the column in line abreast, with at least five yards between each man."

It was so ordered and, after many days of riding in a column of twos formation, it looked rather strange to Talbot. It also prevented any conversation. As they rode over the gentle prairie swells, half of the men were out of his sight much of the time as they disappeared into swales. But this formation did have the desired effect of diffusing the thick dust cloud. And Talbot welcomed the fresher air he was able to breathe.

Within two miles the trail began to broaden and become more pronounced. To Talbot, it appeared some sodbuster had turned about twenty furrows with a bulltongue plow, then harrowed the broken soil into a broad highway.

The men were halted once more while the leaders conferred. Talbot edged his mount close enough to be able to hear nearly all of what was said. John Hurst, a rugged, muscular scout, Grover, Sergeant McCall, Lieutenant Beecher, and Major Forsyth sat their saddles. "Look at that trail, sir," the lieutenant said. "We've found what we've been looking for. Horses and cattle have been driven along here. You can see where travois dragging heavy loads of tent poles and hides have worn deep ruts into the ground."

"That's the truth of the matter, Major," Hurst concurred. "Looks like they've got their families and dogs with them. Those marks were made by several thousand Injuns and animals."

"That large a bunch can't travel fast," Grover added. "We keep on the pace we're goin', we're sure to catch up to them in a day or so. This ain't just a war party that'll take a few shots at us, then skedaddle. These warriors got all their relations and worldly goods with them. They'll fight like hell to protect 'em."

Some other conversation took place, but the words were whisked away from Talbot's ears by a gust of wind.

Moments later, Talbot was not surprised when the major motioned the column forward. Forsyth knew no fear. But where did bravery stop and foolhardiness begin? How had this man survived the war? Sheer luck, apparently. He glanced to his left where Granger was riding parallel, several yards away. Talbot drew a deep breath. So far, this had been exactly what he'd promised — a paid outing in the beautiful, mostly wild country, with decent weather and food.

But he'd been wrong about one thing — it was beginning to look as if they'd see some Indians after all. And, seeing them was probably not going to be the end of it, if Major George Forsyth had his way.

The column continued to walk their horses the rest of the day, then made camp along the banks of what several of the men thought was a fork of the Arikaree River.

The formation was closed up to a column of twos the next day and proceeded slowly and cautiously, still following the shallow stream. Not an Indian was seen.

By the following day, September 16th, Grover and several experienced scouts knew they were very close to the large body of Indians. Major Forsyth suspected the Indians were aware of the column, and decided to order the troop into camp in early afternoon to rest both men and animals. They were nearly out of provisions.

The pre-dawn chill needled Matt Talbot from sleep. Except for boots, hat, and gun belt, he slept fully clothed, the blanket and clumps of bunchgrass the only padding between his stiffened limbs and the hard ground. He curled into a ball and pulled a corner of the gray, wool Army blanket over his cold nose, shivering himself warm.

Irritated at being awakened so early, he was nonetheless relieved at the fading of a fearful nightmare. In the vivid dream, he was coatless and freezing, struggling through the snowy streets of an unfamiliar city, unable to find his way home.

A prevailing west wind had died at sunset, but dry air prevented frost from forming. *If summer on the ladder lingers, autumn tramples on her fingers.* He smiled, recalling the line of poetry from his schoolboy days. And autumn was fast approaching on the high plains.

How strange the events that caused pieces of a puzzle to fall together just so. If he hadn't convinced Phil Granger to come along on this lark, his friend would be waking up, safe and warm, in the back room of the Fort Harker sutler's store, preparing for another boring day. Talbot had labeled this scouting expedition an adventure. That word was usually associated with pain or discomfort. Only later, from a safe distance, did thrilling, dangerous events become treasured memories.

Now he lay with eyes closed, trying to recapture blessed oblivion. But after a few minutes, he gave up. Always a light sleeper, he knew once his slumber was interrupted, it seldom returned. He cracked his eyelids.

Sooty blackness still wrapped the sleeping camp on the grassy swale. He couldn't see the small stream just to the north, but he could hear men snoring, the shuffling of the horses and mules on the picket line, could distinguish the low voice of Major Forsyth as he conversed with one of the sentries. Granger had said the scouts were certain they were not far from a large body of Indians. "I kin smell 'em, Major," Lewis Farley, one of the experienced plainsmen, had declared.

The cautious commander had ordered the column into an early camp on a grassy slope near a gravelly stream. He had ordered fires extinguished at sunset, and forbade smoking or any unnecessary noise.

"Matt, you awake?" came Granger's low voice from several yards away.

"Yeah." Talbot pulled the blanket from his face. "What time is it?"

"Dunno." A hesitation. "Going on five, I reckon." Another pause. "Damned if I don't feel a lot more rested." It was too dark to see the fair, sunburned face, but Talbot could hear his friend groaning as he got up and stretched. "We had all night in for a change," Granger continued. "No sentry duty."

Talbot sat up, rubbing his eyes and looked

58

toward the east. Just above the swell of tree-less prairie, the horizon was aglow, red sky heralding the coming of the sun. " 'Rosy-fingered dawn,' " he muttered, just loud enough for Granger to hear.

"What? Oh, another quote from literature, I guess."

"*The Iliad* or *The Odyssey.* I forget which. Maybe both."

"A good education wasted on this wilderness," Granger said. "Maybe if I hang around with you long enough, some of that will rub off on me. When we met back in Missouri, you got me interested enough to start reading for entertainment. Have to admit, I'm enjoying it. I even tackled *The Odyssey* you recommended. Didn't finish before I had to return the book and move on to another job."

"The gentle undulations of open land look like swells on 'the wine-dark sea.' "

"Same source, I suppose?"

"Yeah. Homer's clichés."

"You ever seen the Mediterranean?"

"Nope. But I hope to someday. Spent six weeks on the North Atlantic when my mother and I came to America during the Great Hunger. A mighty big ocean. I was only five years old, but I can still remember how seasick she was a good bit of the time.

She was skinny as a fence rail." The scene from nineteen years before was vivid in his mind's eye. No sense repeating what he'd previously told Granger about his background in the old country — his father and two siblings dead of starvation in a Kerry County poorhouse, he and his mother fleeing to America with a few pounds for fare donated by an uncle. "I was scared she'd die and leave me alone," he said. "Many's the day I expected the sea to swallow up that old Black Ball packet and take us all to the bottom. You know, Ulysses had the same fear a few times."

Granger stood, stamping his feet into his boots. "I don't recollect Ulysses and his men facing any hostile Injuns."

"Indians might not be as bad as some of the things they did meet on their way home," Talbot said, strapping on his holstered Army Colt and leather cartridge box.

Gray light was stealing over the camp as the men began to stir.

"I got a different quote for you," Granger said quietly, looking east where the red glow resembled a far-off prairie fire. " 'Red sky at morning, sailor take warning.' "

Talbot could see his friend's face in the growing light.

"You think we'll really run into some Injuns?" Granger asked.

"Naw. The major's jumpy and not taking any chances . . . hobbling the horses, doubling the guard on the pack mules, throwing the sentries farther out on the perimeter, forbidding fires. He's been in battle, but he doesn't have any experience with Indians. You can bet if there're any in the vicinity, they know where we are and will stay out of range. If we do come on them, I reckon we'll parlay, since there're only a few of us."

"I hope you're right." Granger turned as Sergeant McCall walked past. "Hey, Sarge, no coffee this morning?"

"No fires means no coffee . . . unless you want to chew the beans," McCall snapped. "Eat cooked rations out of your saddlebags." He moved off, boosting sleeping forms with a boot toe. "Up and out of it! Let's go. Reveille!"

"Grumpy cuss," Granger remarked.

"Probably didn't get much sleep," Talbot said, throwing the saddle blanket over the back of his picketed horse and smoothing it into place.

Granger reached for his McClellan on the ground. "With no tents or cooking fires, we'll be on the move as soon as there's light enough to see. Don't reckon they'll take time to let us bathe in that stream."

Talbot sniffed the sour odor of dried sweat in his own shirt. A bath would be welcome. "Following up that heavy trail today?" He rubbed a hand across the stubble on his lean cheeks.

"Yeah. The major seems to be spoilin' for a fight. Lord knows, that don't make a lot of sense to me," Granger said. "He'd best be sending a couple of fast couriers back to Fort Hays for reinforcements if there are as many Injuns in those combined tribes as Grover and the others seem to think. Small war parties are probably making forays out from the main encampment to kill settlers, burn ranches, and generally raise hell, stealing stock and such. In between, they're following the migrating buffalo, trying to lay in a supply of meat and hides before winter."

"Where the hell are we, anyway?"

"Maps I've seen of this region are pretty sketchy. Not sure even experienced scouts, like Sharp Grover, know the names of some of these creeks, or where they run."

"Yeah. I heard Donovan and Burke calling this the South Fork of the Republican. Grover seems to think it's the Arikaree. Farley says it's Delaware Creek. One thing about it . . . we're a damned long way from anywhere civilized."

As he cinched up, Talbot noticed Lieutenant Frederick Beecher pause nearby to have a word with one of the men. The competent officer was so popular that head scout Sharp Grover stated he would agree to ride on this patrol only if Lieutenant Beecher was second in command. Several of the other experienced plainsmen seconded that notion, so Major Forsyth had requested the lieutenant's services.

Beecher limped away and took hold of the mount one of the scouts had saddled for him. "Shot in the knee at Gettysburg. Lucky he didn't lose the leg. But the damage is permanent," Granger said, watching the lieutenant.

"Not as permanent as it could've been," Talbot said. "Or as total."

Talbot and Granger fished in their saddlebags for half-cooked strips of bacon to chew on. The salty meat was the best thing Talbot had tasted for some time. He found himself wishing he had scrambled eggs, biscuits, and coffee to go with the cold, limp bacon. His belly had flattened to the point where he had to take up an extra notch in his belt.

In a silent explosion of light the sun finally cleared the horizon. Talbot welcomed the warmth it would bring within the hour. By noon they'd be sweating.

Two gunshots shattered the quiet morning.

Lewis Farley and Major Forsyth ran toward camp from the northern perimeter. "Stand to horses! Rifles at the ready!" Forsyth yelled. "Indians!"

Talbot looked where Farley was pointing, but saw nothing above the edge of the rise to the west. He grabbed the Spencer carbine out of the loop on the saddle. He always kept its tubular magazine fully loaded with seven .56-caliber cartridges. Their horses, accustomed to the noise of gunfire, had not shied. Even so, Talbot had the presence of mind not to kick the picket pin out of the hard earth just yet.

The seasoned men sprang to their mounts and stood ready for orders, some holding their mounts up short with braided lariats.

A war party of Indians came riding out of a ravine upstream, whooping and rattling dried hides and beating small drums, trying to stampede the horses and mules.

Several Spencers erupted in flame, and the raiders retreated to cover.

"Look to the horses!" Lieutenant Beecher yelled.

The major and the sentry came up, panting. Martin Burke and two other men were leading in the pack mules and spare horses that had been picketed. "They ran off five mules!" Burke yelled.

"How the hell did that happen?" Forsyth demanded. "Didn't you have them secured?"

"Sorry, sir. We'd taken off the hobbles and had them on picket, ready to lash on the packs and head out. Hurst held *these* animals just by main strength. But the heathens didn't get the mules with food or ammunition," Burke added.

The six foot, five Hurst was tugging the lead ropes of three mules.

"Heavens, Major, look. . . ." Sharp Grover touched Forsyth's shoulder and pointed.

A breathless silence fell over the group.

On the skyline of the rise some three hundred yards away, horsemen were appearing — in twos and threes, then dozens. They seemed to spring, fully armed, out of the very earth. From up and down the sandy riverbed, from across the stream and along the opposite bank, from the rising ground back of the camp, and fore and aft of the scouts on this side of the river, hundreds of warriors materialized. With a low rumble of hoofs, they started into view from all sides, and paused, just out of effective carbine range, an unbroken fringe of paint ponies and painted brown bodies, eagle feather war bonnets waving in the early morning breeze, the rising sun glinting from lance points and rifle barrels.

Forsyth grabbed the field glasses Lieutenant Beecher uncased and studied the distant apparition for several long seconds.

Talbot's mouth and throat went dry; he couldn't speak. He wanted to reach for his canteen on the saddle, but seemed frozen in place.

"Gawd," Granger breathed. "There must be six, seven hundred of 'em. You reckon they come to bring us our morning coffee?" He gave a sickly grin.

Talbot felt the bottom fall out of his stomach.

CHAPTER FIVE

Grover swept his gaze in a circle around them. "Major, we're outnumbered at least ten to one."

"And they've blocked the way we came up the valley," Forsyth replied. "If we try to run, they'll cut us down in the open."

Jack Stilwell, a curly-haired nineteen-year-old scout spoke up: "Major, we could hunker down on that island yonder." He pointed at the long, brushy sandbar in the middle of the river opposite their camp.

Talbot looked at this suggested refuge. The island was about a hundred yards long and maybe fifty across. Near the upstream end stood a lone cottonwood, with a trunk barely a foot thick. The rest of the island bristled with scrub bushes, plum thickets, and waist-high grass.

"Nothing there that'll stop a bullet, but it's our best chance," Forsyth said. "Move onto that island, men!" he ordered.

"Let's go!"

The scouts led their horses across, churning up the foot-deep stream.

"Get a good grip on those two mules!" Sergeant McCall yelled. "They're packing our spare ammunition."

As if on cue, one of the mules balked at wading into the water, and sat down on his haunches. Muleskinner Asa Conklin tugged at the bridle while another man stung the animal's withers with the end of a rawhide lariat. Finally the braying mule lunged upward and trotted into the water with Conklin still clinging to the headstall.

On the crest of the rises, a few shots popped from Indian rifles, but the shooters were effectively out of range.

From downstream, a solid phalanx of bronzed riders began trotting their mounts toward the island. They were still three hundred yards away.

"Tie your horses in a circle!" Lieutenant Beecher shouted. "Get down inside the circle and dig in!"

Grover ran up to Forsyth. "Major, let me take four or five men and hide out in that long grass hanging over the cutbanks on both sides of the river. When those redskins jump their horses down over the bank to the streambed, we can damn' near touch 'em with our carbines."

"Pick your men and get to it," Forsyth said, taking the reins of Grover's horse.

"Harrington! Murphy! Johnson! Bledsoe!" Grover shouted. "Tie up your horses and come with me!"

The five men dashed across the shallow bar and Grover motioned three to the far side of the river, while he and Bledsoe hid themselves under the long grass on the near side.

Talbot and Granger mounted and splashed their horses across the stream and up into the brush of the island. Talbot's heart was pounding, but he moved with deliberation.

"I hate to fight with wet, cold feet," Granger said, dismounting and snubbing his mount to a sapling. "I was wet and muddy and cold during the whole damned war. Vowed I'd never be that way again if I could help it." He pulled a tin plate from his saddlebags, dropped to his hands and knees, and began digging.

Talbot yanked his sheath knife and joined him, stabbing, chopping, and ripping at the grass, the thin soil, and the sand underneath. Men all around were digging furiously with whatever tools they could find. Dirt and gravel flew as they panted, scraped, and scooped, piling up the detritus to form a lip around the narrow trenches.

In all the seeming confusion and haste, a hurried order was apparent. Two men unloaded the two big boxes of ammunition, pried off the wooden lids, and laid out packets of cartridges within easy reach. The experienced men among them were instructing the others about digging the slender rifle pits so they could lie, facing outward from a central point. The work went swiftly and Talbot sensed the desperation. If they were all to be overrun and killed, at least he wouldn't die alone. It was cold comfort. He pushed the thought away and concentrated on the job at hand. They had only a couple of minutes.

"Be ready, boys!" came the major's calm voice as he strolled among them, leading his horse with one hand and gripping a revolver in the other. "They're starting an attack. Make every shot count. Don't waste ammunition. Our lives could depend on it."

Talbot grabbed his Spencer from the ground and wiggled into the cool, damp gravel of the shallow trench he'd managed to scrape out. There was a round in the chamber of his weapon so he didn't work the loading lever. But he had to use both hands to thumb back the hammer. "What's wrong with my hands?" he muttered aloud. They were trembling so violently, he could hardly control them.

Then, he was suddenly conscious of gunshots around him, and wondered how his mind could have blocked out the sound until now.

"Hold your fire until they're closer, boys," the major said, still strolling among the trenches. He'd tied his horse to help form part of the wide circle. "Pay no mind to those Indians on both sides. They're too far away on the hills. The charge will come from there." He pointed downstream.

The scouts looked to their weapons as they all turned toward the lower end of the island. Talbot noted grim determination on the bearded and wind-burned faces of the scouts as they gripped their Spencers. In the sudden stillness, Talbot heard the low rumble of hundreds of unshod hoofs. The phalanx of attackers was at least sixty riders wide and six or eight deep. While he gazed toward the distant horsemen who filled the shallow river valley from side to side, they broke from a trot into a full gallop, sweeping toward the low-lying sandbar.

He glanced to one side at Granger several feet away, also lying prone in a shallow rifle pit. To make an even smaller target of

71

himself, he'd removed his hat. Granger looked up and grinned, although his fair face was pale beneath the sunburn. "We got 'em just where we want 'em." The rest of his comment was lost in a barrage of gunfire as Spencers all around erupted in blasts of flame. Bullets were beginning to zip through the bushes. The horses plunged and squealed as lead struck them. Two of the panicked animals broke loose and went charging away.

"Get down, Major!" Dr. Mooers entreated the commander as Forsyth was still walking upright, his voice barely heard above the uproar. "Be calm, boys! Take your time and aim low! If you don't hit the rider, you'll get his horse!"

The major's calm demeanor had an effect. Talbot noted his hands had stopped shaking. He took a deep breath. If Forsyth thought they'd be all right, then he had to believe it as well.

The charge was within a hundred yards of the lower end of the island. Would that line of horsemen ride right over them? Talbot's finger tightened on the trigger that had a substantial pull. Even though the sun had cleared the rise to the east, it was difficult to pick out individual moving targets through the tall grass, thick bushes, and their own horses' legs constantly shifting. He lined up his sights on a bare, painted breast. It disappeared behind an obstruction. He swung his sights to pick up another coming straight at him. He pulled the trigger and the Spencer slammed back into his shoulder. He jacked open the lever, flipping out the empty shell, and yanked the breech closed, seating another cartridge. He fired again, not waiting to see the result of his shot. Indians were close now, horses were going down, kicking, somersaulting riders over their heads, or landing atop those Indians who'd tied themselves on. War cries mingled with the constant roar of gunfire from both sides. Bullets kicked up sand all around. Talbot's horse staggered two steps and fell, nearly landing on top of him. A slug had struck the animal in the forehead.

"You bastards! Shoot my horse, will ya!" He was hardly aware that he fired seven times until the hammer fell on an empty chamber. The barrel was too hot to touch. He laid the weapon aside and fumbled for his belted ammunition box to reload. Cartridges dropped from his fingers as he hastened to shove them into the hollow tube he extracted from the butt stock. In his peripheral vision, he saw two scouts slump and roll over, one yelling with pain.

But the scouts were exacting a toll, too. Sergeant McCall yelled for them to fire in volleys, instead of individually. At the third volley, the charge faltered and broke, the line of ponies and riders splitting to go around either side of the island. The attackers swept by within thirty yards, hanging off the sides of their ponies to fire under the animals' necks. Gunfire from the hillsides ceased as the stationary Indian riflemen couldn't take a chance on hitting their companions.

"Hold your fire, men! Wait till you have a good target!" Forsyth shouted.

"Get down, Major!"

"Uh!" Forsyth staggered and fell, clutching his right thigh. "I'm hit."

The doctor pulled the commander into his own rifle pit. "Let me see."

In the process of rolling over, Forsyth crooked his left leg upward. A slug slammed into his left shin. "Oh, my God. My other leg's broke," Forsyth gasped.

Dr. Mooers and another scout eased the major into the rifle pit. The doctor sat up and leaned over to examine the wounds.

Thwack!

Dr. Mooers fell forward without a sound, blood oozing from a hole in his forehead.

"*Aw,* shit! They got Doc!" a scout yelled.

"Damn it! I ain't gonna stay here and be shot down like a hog in a pen!" the scout cried in a high-pitched voice that cut through every other sound. "Anybody want to make a dash with me to the far bank?"

"Hell, yes," a voice answered. "Let's go."

"I'm with you!" Talbot yelled, eager for any kind of positive action.

Three more men scrambled to join them.

"Stay where you are!" Forsyth ordered in a deadly tone, brandishing his Colt. "I'll shoot down any man who attempts to leave this island." Sweat beaded on his pain-wracked face, but his blue eyes blazed.

The two scouts froze halfway to their feet and sank back into their rifle pits.

"If he doesn't shoot you, I will," Sergeant McCall snarled, hard eyes locking on Talbot's.

"You bent-nose bastard," Talbot hissed under his breath.

"What'd you say?" Sergeant Jake McCall grabbed Talbot's shirt front and jerked him close.

Talbot whacked the arm away with his carbine barrel. "Don't threaten me!" He swung up the Spencer.

A look of pure hate crawled across McCall's brutal features. His eyes narrowed, thick lips compressed. He thumbed back the hammer of his Colt.

"Enough!" barked Forsyth. "Talbot, you and every one of these civilian scouts signed on to accept military command."

"You addle-brained idiots," Lieutenant Beecher added in a milder tone. "Leaving here would be the worst thing you could do. We're surrounded and outnumbered. If we panic and scatter, they'll shoot us down like a covey of quail. Our only chance is to stick together and hunker down right here."

During the lull, Indians scrambled to retrieve their dead and wounded. Riderless horses and ponies were plunging wildly along the gravel streambed. The scouts didn't dare rise up from their trenches for fear of being shot by the riflemen on both sides of the river who were apparently creeping closer and getting the range.

During the few minutes of relative silence, Talbot heard only the scraping of makeshift tools deepening the trenches, along with the eerie keening of death chants in the distance.

Granger tugged the saddle off a nearby dead horse. "This here hickory saddle tree'll stop more lead than all the bushes on this island," he grunted, tilting the saddle up on the edge of his depression and thrusting the barrel of his carbine through the slot in the seat. "Perfect rifle port."

It was a sunny, cool morning, but Talbot was damp with sweat. He was able to reach the canteen on the saddle of his dead mount and took a long drink. Finally capping the canteen, he wiped his face with a sleeve and drew a deep breath. He had no illusions that the Indians were through with them. This was only the beginning, yet already he was fatigued from the strain. If he didn't drop dead from exhaustion, a bullet would probably end his life. Every man on this island would be dead before sunset. They were only prolonging the inevitable. Fatalistic, he thought, but realistic. There was no way this handful of scouts could survive long with limited ammunition and no food.

How would he die? He'd never let himself be captured; he'd force the Indians to kill him outright. The torture these primitives could devise was legendary, and he shuddered at the remembrance of the two mutilated and scalped Mexican teamsters he'd seen at the freight wagons.

He glanced over at Granger who was reloading his Spencer; his grim expression suddenly brightened up. "What's an outing without a little pepper sauce on the vittles?" he asked.

"I promised you adventure." Talbot

grinned. "I finally delivered."

In the heat of action, with adrenaline pumping, he had no time to reflect. Desperation crowded out all other thoughts. But now the minutes began dragging like a broken travois. He had to be mentally tough and use the lull to prepare himself for the next attack.

He was distracted by a shout and scattered shots. Grover and the four other scouts were floundering across the shallows toward the shelter of the island. The five men slid inside the broken circle of dead horses, rolling into the rifle pits.

"We plugged a few of 'em, Major . . . ," Grover panted. "Handy as shootin' fish in a barrel. But now they got us spotted. Had to get out."

One of Grover's men, Frank Harrington, streaked with blood from head to knees, wiped some of it from his face. "Caught an arrow above the right eye," he said.

Black-haired Tom Murphy crept up to him. "Don't look like it penetrated the bone. I tried to yank it out, but the damned shaft came off in me hand. The stone point is stuck."

"Look out!"

A mounted warrior crashed through the brush, firing pointblank at Harrington as the horse leaped over them and was gone before anyone could react.

Harrington flopped over on his side, but popped back up, hand to his head. His hand came away bloody, revealing a flap of skin where the arrowhead had been.

Murphy took a closer look. "Well, I'll be damned! Your guardian angel's looking out for you today, Harrington. That bullet knocked the arrowhead right out of your thick skull." He pulled a flask from inside his jacket and poured a trickle over the gash. The wounded man jerked back with a gasp. "You trying to burn me up with that there whiskey?" he cried.

"Hate to waste me precious stock on you," Murphy said. "But, like a magic elixir, it'll keep the wound from festering while it heals." He capped the flask. "Now, if those red devils will give me half a minute, I'll get a bandage on that before you leak out your life's blood into your shoes. I've never seen a living man so bloody." He proceeded to rip off his own shirt tail and fashion a crude bandage around Harrington's head.

"September Seventeenth is a day I'll remember the rest of my life," Harrington said, pushing up the bandage away from his eyes.

"I hope the rest of your life is later than

tomorrow," Murphy said.

"They're forming up again, Major," Lieutenant Beecher announced, staring through the field glasses toward the upper end of the island. "And it looks like Roman Nose is leading the charge this time." He handed the glasses to Forsyth who was propped up on one elbow in his rifle pit. "He's the big, naked savage in the middle," Beecher said. "One feather in his hair. He's a good deal over six feet tall and weighs at least two-twenty. Kind of a hooked nose."

"I see him," Forsyth said, lowering the glasses. "Looks like most of them are back in the shelter of that cut to the right. They'll come out of there and attack from upstream. They won't have far to come to the head of the island." He handed the glasses back to his second in command. "Get the men ready. Be sure their carbines are fully loaded. Have them fire in volleys again. That seems to work best." Forsyth grimaced in pain from his wounded legs and leaned back against the saddle. The comatose doctor lay on a blanket near his feet. Nothing could be done for him.

Sergeant McCall passed the word to face upstream and prepare to repel the charge.

From Talbot's point of view, low in the rifle pit, not much could be seen through the thick screen of grass and brush. A jumble of horses and riders, then a war whoop and the vibration of a thousand hoofs. A few seconds later he could see the torsos of the warriors above the tangle and picked out a giant Indian in front he assumed was Roman Nose. The Indian was shaking his heavy Sharps overhead with one hand.

A Spencer exploded a few feet away.

"Not yet," Sergeant McCall snapped. "I'll give the command."

The rumble grew louder. Talbot held his breath, hammer cocked, finger off the trigger.

"Up on one knee!" the sergeant called.

The scouts sprang into position, leaning forward, bracing their weapons.

"Not yet . . . not yet . . . *now!*"

Four dozen carbines crashed in unison.

The wave of attackers kept coming.

Levers ratcheted.

"Ready . . . *now!*"

A sheet of flame lanced from the carbine muzzles.

The attackers seemed to falter, but were only two hundred feet from the head of the island.

"Ready . . . *now!*"

Spencers roared.

Riders and horses tumbled onto the sandbar. Others swept up onto the island past the lone cottonwood and kept coming.

"Get down, men!" McCall's shout was almost drowned in the thunder of gunfire. Bullets were zipping through the brush, kicking up spouts of sand. Two men dropped into their pits, then another fell forward on his face.

"Ready . . . now!"

From a prone position, the scouts' blasted a volley that shattered the air like a single cannon. More Indians tumbled.

The next wave of hot lead brought down Roman Nose and his horse; both of which pitched down and out of Talbot's sight.

The leader's fall seemed to break the attack. The charge faltered and the remaining riders veered off and galloped back upstream at full speed, the painted warriors lying low over their ponies' backs.

"Stay down!" Sergeant McCall yelled. The Indians who'd crept closer downslope from both sides of the river now had a clear field of fire with the attackers out of the way. Apparently furious at the loss of Roman Nose, they cut loose a withering fire on the island from both banks of the river. Lead bullets splattered into dead horseflesh, and zinged off saplings and tore grooves in the earth as the men hugged the bottoms of their shallow trenches. But their shooting did little damage, as far as Talbot could tell. It slacked off after about two minutes. Four flaming arrows arced overhead to land in the dry grass. But they were ineffective at starting fires due to the damp sand and the scouts who quickly smothered them.

Talbot's ears were ringing. He couldn't touch his carbine barrel without burning his fingers. He found himself gasping for air and realized he'd been holding his breath. For the moment, danger had passed, but he knew the scouts couldn't withstand many more assaults like that.

The angle of the sun showed it to be about 2:00 P.M. The day seemed endless. If they could last until dark, would the Indians attack at night? He sucked down the last of the tepid water in his canteen. It did little to slake his thirst. He could have drunk a gallon without stopping.

A light breeze brought the sound of high-pitched wailing atop a low bluff to the north where women had gathered to watch the battle. Bodies of their husbands, sons, and brothers dotted the sandy riverbed.

Using his carbine as a crutch, Lieutenant Beecher rose from his trench and staggered a few yards to Forsyth's pit. He slumped down, took a deep breath, and gasped: "I have my death wound, Major. I'm shot in the side." He laid his head down on his forearm.

"No, Beecher," Forsyth said. "It can't be as bad as that."

"Yes . . . good night." With that, he sagged into the pit next to his commander. Although Talbot could see his chest rising and falling, it seemed only a matter of time. The side of his tunic was a mass of blood.

While the lull continued, Grover crawled over to the pale, sweating Forsyth and said: "Sir, let me take a few men and sweep up to the head of the island. I know there're some Indians who dropped off in that brush and mean to ambush us."

Forsyth nodded. "Go ahead, but don't take unnecessary chances. We can't afford to lose any more men."

In less than a minute, Grover had his volunteers and the men crept away into the thick grass and bushes, carrying only their loaded revolvers and knives.

A few minutes later Talbot heard struggling and grunting and a sharp cry. He looked at Granger. Two shots exploded. More scrabbling in the brush. Shortly Grover and his men returned. "We got two of them," he reported to the major. "The rest got away."

Hours ground along with the deliberation of a mill wheel. Indians gathered the bodies of their dead they could reach without coming into range.

The scouts also took advantage of the slack to lay out their own dead and cover them with blankets. Weapons of the deceased were distributed among the able-bodied, and loaded for the next attack.

Forsyth ordered the saddles removed from the dead horses and used to fortify their breastworks. The others busied themselves deepening their trenches. Two feet was considered minimum. One of the younger scouts with a Bowie knife actually struck water more than three feet down in the sandy soil. This was a welcome find, and the muddy water was filtered through a clean bandanna to fill all the canteens that were passed over.

"Cut steaks off those dead animals," Forsyth ordered, still in charge, although frequently faint from extreme pain and blood loss. "Eat what you can, then wrap the rest and bury them in the sand so they won't spoil as fast."

"Too bad those first attackers got away with the mules that had our provisions," Talbot said.

"We ate the last of our food yesterday," Granger answered. "Warn't nothin' on them mules but salt and coffee and a few pots and pans. We're damned lucky they didn't get the mules carrying the extra ammunition."

Talbot and Granger busied themselves deepening and connecting their rifle pits. The other scouts were doing the same to form a network of trenches.

At 6:00 that evening another attack came. The Indians formed in the same deep bend upstream and came galloping down the riverbed toward the island, yelling and shooting. But the scouts, now toughened by the earlier assaults and protected by their deeper trenches, were able to pick out targets coolly and drop the attackers with more accurate shots as they came within range. The charge broke and the Indians scattered before reaching the end of the island.

Talbot sipped water from his canteen. It was cool, but tasted like dirt. He crawled out of his trench and, without rising, stretched his arms and legs as best he could. He felt as if he'd been in a knockdown fight. His muscles were stiff and sore from being tensed for hours.

Granger looked up from gnawing on a

hunk of bloody horse meat. "This situation almost makes me homesick for that dull sutler's store," he said, attempting a grin.

The sun was going down behind a streaked pall of clouds. The westerly breeze, drying sweat on his body, brought a fresh smell of rain.

"Bite of steak?" Granger offered the red meat.

"No thanks." Talbot felt a bit queasy. "Too rare for me. I think that dirty water upset my stomach."

"I'm gonna spread my slicker in this here hole and catch some o' the rain that's coming. It's been hotter'n hell today. A shower's gonna feel almighty refreshing."

Am I the only one who ever thinks of dying? Talbot wondered, sliding back into his trench. Perhaps these silent men around him were being tortured at this moment by such fears. Likely some of these hardened frontiersmen lived such rough lives, they'd come to accept death as naturally as they did the everyday pain of living, and never gave it a thought. If such were the case, they were more like animals than men. To Talbot, thinking and reflecting on the nature of life and the universe seemed more akin to human nature than a simple, naturalistic existence. Sensitivity, however, certainly opened a man to more anguish.

None of the white men lying in these grimy rifle pits on a gravel bar in the middle of a stream on a vast prairie was liable to see the sun come up again. Yet, here was the practical Granger, eating what food there was, and planning to catch rain water, as if this were just another rough spot on the road to paradise.

CHAPTER SIX

Two hours later an early darkness came down over the little island, and a light rain began to fall. Talbot lay in his trench, uncovered, relishing the cooling shower on his overheated body.

McCall crept among the trenches. "Major Forsyth is looking for a volunteer to sneak out and go for help," he announced in a hoarse whisper. He repeated his message several times before a youthful voice came out of the darkness. "I'll give it a try." It was nineteen-year-old Jack Stilwell.

"Thank God for young men," Granger said quietly to Talbot. "They always seem to think they're indestructible."

"Young Indians, too," Talbot whispered back. "Grover says the young bucks are eager to fight." He could see the murky forms of Stilwell and McCall moving past him toward Forsyth's pit a few feet away.

"Think you can slip through this circle of

Indians and go for help to Fort Wallace?" Forsyth's voice sounded low but clear nearby.

"I'll give it a shot," Stilwell replied.

"The fort's about a hundred ten miles south by east of here. I'll give you my only map."

"Before dark I built a fire in one of the pits and roasted strips of horse meat to stuff into your pockets," McCall said.

Stilwell and Forsyth exchanged a few more words, when suddenly another, rougher voice spoke up. "Hell, I can't let the kid go alone. I got plenty experience with Indians. I'll go with him."

"Trudeau, get over here," McCall said. "I might've figured you'd deal yourself in on this."

"Hell, I don't figure we got much chance if we stay here," Pierre Trudeau said. The forty-year-old plainsman moved, cat-like, in the darkness and hunkered down between Talbot and Forsyth.

"Take only a pistol, full cartridge box, and canteen each," Forsyth said. "I'll write a note to the post commander."

"OK, now listen, kid," Trudeau said. "We'll take off our boots, tie 'em together, and hang 'em around our neck. We'll stay in the riverbed as long as we can and then see how tight they got the sentries around us."

"Better wait until after midnight and hope the rain picks up," Stilwell said.

"Good thinking."

Talbot lay in his rifle pit, listening to their plans. It was a long shot they could even break out of the ring, much less walk over a hundred miles on the open plains without being seen and killed. But desperate circumstances called for desperate measures.

He could see Indian fires winking on the low hills. When the patter of rain increased to a steady, soaking volume, he pulled a slicker over himself, but the water just ran down into the trench and wet him from beneath.

Apathy overcame him. His mind was in a fog. From experience, he knew this was a result of fatigue brought on by hours of stress and heat. If he ate something to restore his energy, he'd feel better. But raw horse meat and dirty water had no appeal, even if he'd been hungry. Wasn't much point in food, if he was about to die. Would the Indians sneak up on them in the darkness, their movements masked by the falling rain? He didn't relish having his throat slashed while he slept. Better to go down fighting in daylight with his companions all around. If Stilwell and Trudeau did, by some miracle, get through, how long would it take for help to arrive? Ten days or two weeks, probably. By then, it wouldn't matter.

To keep from concentrating on himself, he thought of Major Forsyth. Their leader had been wounded twice in the legs. In spite of his obvious pain, the major was still calmly in command. Several men were dead and more than ten wounded. Sergeant McCall had assigned men for sentry duty through the night to prevent a possible surprise attack. But neither of the professional soldiers believed these Indians would attack at night. Word had been passed through the group an hour before that Lieutenant Beecher had died. And Dr. Mooers lay mortally wounded. Talbot knew in his heart this would be the fate of them all. There was no other possibility. They were surrounded, far outnumbered, isolated in a remote area a hundred miles from the nearest military post, and out of food except for spoiling horse meat and dirty water.

In spite of their successive attacks and superior numbers, the Indians had failed to ride over and annihilate the little band. Perhaps the Indians would now change tactics and settle in for a long siege to starve them out, or pick them off one and two at a time if they tried to escape. In any case, the end was inevitable.

Grimy, unshaven, wet, he was so exhausted, he fell into a doze. Fearful, bloody dreams disturbed his subconscious before he slid into the oblivion of deep slumber — his temporary escape.

Talbot awoke disoriented. Then the horror of their situation rushed back on him. Daylight was streaking the eastern sky. Lying on his back, he watched the rain clouds blowing away to the east. He pushed off the slicker and rolled over. Other men were stirring. A dozen feet away, Major Forsyth sat propped against a saddle, a hand on his wounded thigh. He didn't appear to have slept, judging from his haggard, red-eyed look.

Talbot glanced the other way at Granger who was sitting up in his trench. " 'Mornin'," his friend greeted him, raking fingers through his disheveled blond hair.

"Sleep well?"

"I don't recommend the accommodations of this hotel," Granger said. "Although I guess I could have slept on a bed of nails."

"I'm some better," Talbot said. "What's for breakfast?" His stomach was growling.

"Same as . . . raw horse and water."

"I'll take it."

Granger unwrapped a hunk of red meat from a saturated cotton bag that had once held a side of bacon.

Talbot wiped off his knife blade and sliced off a fist-sized chunk. "Pass the salt."

"How about some potatoes and bread, too?"

"Never mind. As the old saying goes, hunger makes the best sauce." In spite of his earlier aversion, he ate the meat with a good appetite and felt much better for it afterward.

"Hey, Sarge, did Stilwell and Trudeau get through?" a scout called.

"Hope so. Didn't hear any shooting in the night," McCall replied.

"They could just as likely be lying out there in the river with their throats cut and their scalps gone," Granger muttered.

Talbot would've preferred not to contemplate that image with his breakfast.

"Talbot!" came Major Forsyth's voice. "You and Granger come here."

Talbot wiped his mouth and approached the officer, surprised the major even knew his name.

"You handle that knife pretty well," Forsyth said, tight-lipped, looking at Talbot. "I want you to cut out this slug."

"Sir, I'm not a doctor."

"We have no doctor now. But I was watching you slice that meat. You have a steady hand."

If he only knew, Talbot thought, recalling how he was shaking before the battle started.

Forsyth's trouser leg was torn and stained with dried blood. "Bullet went in just above the knee," the major went on as if Talbot had consented to take it out. "Came up this way . . ." — he traced the path with his finger — "and lodged just below the surface here, inside my thigh." He pressed down the flesh with his thumbs. "See the lump? It's giving me fits and I want it out of there. You can do it."

"Sir, I. . . ." He swallowed and tried again. "That bullet's awfully close to the femoral artery. If I slip just a little, you could bleed to death," Talbot said, cringing at disobeying an order, but willing to risk any admonishment to keep from taking such a risk.

"Well, I can't leave it in there any longer," Forsyth said, reaching into his saddlebags behind him. He brought out a small case containing a straight razor.

Talbot and Granger glanced at each other as the major began stropping the blade on his leather boot. Was he going to operate on himself?

The commander honed the edge to his satisfaction, then pressed down tentatively on the flesh of his thigh with his left hand until the lump of lead bullet showed clearly. "Press your fingers right here," he ordered.

Talbot did as instructed, flattening the heavy thigh muscle around the bullet.

Forsyth drew a deep, ragged breath and touched the lump with a stroke of the blade. The bullet almost popped out, followed by a flow of blood.

"Murphy . . . give me your flask," Forsyth said. He dribbled a little on the wound. "*Whew,* that feels a good deal better already." He sighed, blotting the blood with his bandanna.

"Major, you want to keep this for a souvenir?" Granger asked, holding out the bloody bullet.

"I reckon not." A tight smile showed below his mustache. "But I'll take the one that got Roman Nose, if you can find it. Bringing down that big bastard really took the heart out of them."

"We ain't off the griddle by a long way," Grover said, worming his way close enough to hear the last of the conversation. "But killing Roman Nose let 'em know their medicine ain't as strong as they thought."

"Sergeant McCall!"

"Sir?"

"How many dead and wounded?"

Talbot moved away, relieved to be no longer the focus of the major's attention. Before he was out of earshot, he heard McCall giving an account of casualties.

"Not counting Lieutenant Beecher, Doctor Mooers, and yourself, sir, Chalmers, Smith, and Wilson are dead or dying. Scouts Louis Farley and Bernie Day are mortally wounded. O'Donnell, Davis, Tucker, Gantt, Clarke, Armstrong, Morton, and Violette are severely wounded." He consulted a notebook in his hand. "Slightly wounded . . . Harrington, Davenport, Haley, McLaughlin, Hudson, McPhee, and two others whose names I didn't get."

"So we have seven dead and eight severely wounded who are out of action."

"Yes, sir."

The sun had cleared the horizon. As if on signal, the Indian marksmen opened a sporadic fire from the low hills.

"*Ahh!*" Major Forsyth jerked and flopped onto his back.

"Damn!" McCall sprang to the wounded man's side.

"Major! George!" He pulled away the torn hat, but no blood showed on the head.

Talbot's stomach clenched while he watched McCall feel for a pulse in Forsyth's throat.

"He's still alive."

"Where was he hit?"

"Don't know." McCall picked up the major's hat and ran his finger through holes in the brim and the crown.

Forsyth's eyes flickered open. For a moment, he stared at the sky, then focused on McCall. "Damn, Sergeant, my head must be harder than the men say."

"Bullet must've caught you a glancing blow," McCall said, parting the major's hair just above the temple.

"Careful!" Forsyth flinched.

"Gonna have a real goose egg there," the sergeant said. "It's already swelling."

"Not to mention one helluva headache." The major groaned, gingerly touching his head.

"Wonder if those Indian sharpshooters got the range on you?" McCall said.

"Dumb luck," Forsyth replied.

"Maybe. But they could know you're a chief. You and I might be special targets since we're the only ones wearing blue uniforms. They already got Lieutenant Beecher," McCall said, handing the major his hat.

Forsyth glanced at the tear in the brim. "This might've saved my life. I had the brim bent back so I could see better. The double thickness of felt absorbed some of the shock of that spent bullet." He eased the hat back on his head. "Feeling woozy. If I black out, you're to assume command. Understand?"

"Yes, sir," McCall said.

"We ain't gonna bury 'em proper, Sarge?" one of the men asked an hour later when McCall was directing the bodies to be wrapped in blankets and moved away from the rifle pits.

"No shovels," McCall said. "And we're still under fire. Just hide the bodies in the brush where the Indians can't get close enough to desecrate them." He gestured skyward where a half dozen black vultures drifted in lazy circles on high thermals. "Don't waste any ammunition on them. They won't bother the bodies as long as they have easy pickins' of all this horse meat."

The men carefully wrapped the bodies and, crawling on hands and knees, dragged them into heavy brush, lining them up, side-by-side.

McCall kept the rest of the scouts busy, either connecting trenches, tending the wounded, or cutting more meat from the dead horses while some of it was still edible.

So far, there was no need to ration ammunition; the pack mules had carried an adequate number of cartridges for an extended siege. Now and then, when an Indian became careless and exposed himself within range, a scout would take a shot at him. The Indians seemed to have plenty of ammunition since they kept up a scattered fire most of the day. But generally, the battle settled into a stand-off and remained that way the rest of the day with no more charges or attempted individual coups. They'd been stung, their leader killed, and individual warriors were now much more circumspect about riding swiftly down on the island to take close up shots at the scouts.

The second night pulled its curtain over the whole scene, relieving the heat of the September sunlight. The shooting ceased and the campfires on the surrounding hills were the only lights to be seen.

"I used to like rare steak," Granger said to Talbot. "But, after this, I think I'll eat mine well done."

"How long do you think we can last?" Talbot asked.

Granger was silent for a long minute. "If

nothing changes, and those Injuns are persistent, I'd guess maybe a week. Not much more."

"Think Forsyth will try to have us bust out of this?"

"I heard McCall say he was going to send out two more couriers tonight in case Stilwell and Trudeau didn't get through. That's about all he can do. Unless we could catch a few of those horses running loose, we're afoot. Forsyth and some of the others are wounded and can't even walk. If we leave this island, we're dead a lot quicker than if we hunker down right here and hope for some miracle."

"Not good news."

"You asked. That's just my guess." He spat out a hunk of meat. "Of course we might die of the bellyache from rotten meat. This stuff is getting more tender every hour, what with that hot sun working on it. I'll be for giving the rest of my share to the buzzards by tomorrow night."

At 11:00 that night, Talbot heard the major instructing scouts, Pliley and Donovan to make a try at breaking out of the cordon. The two men slipped away silently.

The night was clear and cool with no sign of rain. Talbot would have welcomed the warmth of a cheery fire — a fire that would roast some of the remaining meat into something a little tastier. But fires had been forbidden. They would illuminate the men as perfect targets for Indians creeping close under cover of darkness. To make matters worse, he caught a whiff of wood smoke from Indian fires, now and then, along with the delicious aroma of cooking meat.

Talbot lay in his trench and tried to think of something besides food. Shortly before it'd gotten too dark to see, he'd made an entry in his new journal, outlining their situation in terse phrases, trying to stick to the facts without allowing emotion to creep into his words. The whole time he was writing, the thought lurked in the back of his mind that some white man picking through their bones would likely be the next person to read these jottings. His own words, along with whatever Major Forsyth would enter into his personal log, and possibly a few letters left by other scouts, would be the only record of what'd happened here. But no white man would read these recordings until long after it was too late to help.

Should he hide the journal so it wouldn't be found and destroyed by their killers? No. Indians who couldn't read English would have no reason to take this book. They'd consider it trash. He shoved the journal into the pocket of his jacket with the feeling of a man burying a time capsule.

Talbot doffed his jacket and covered himself with it against the chilly night air, then lay down on his blanket in the bottom of the rifle pit. Hours of hot sun had dried out his clothing and all their blankets, so he at least didn't have to endure the discomfort of being wet. Even though he was reasonably comfortable, he was unable to sleep. A few hours later, he heard scuffling nearby and the voices of the Pliley and Donovan reporting to Forsyth they'd been unable to find a way through the surrounding Indians.

Another hope dashed. He wasn't as exhausted as he'd been the night before, so sleep eluded him. Maybe his mind, anticipating what was to come, could not relax. Whatever the cause, he lay on his back and watched the slow wheeling of stars across the firmament. Some of the severely wounded were moaning and muttering nearby. Except for stanching the blood of their wounds and giving them water when conscious, not much could be done for them. One man's forearm and another's leg had been crudely splinted. Of the few men killed, why did one of them have to be their indispensable surgeon? It was only one of the many questions that paraded through his restless mind. Maybe this whole thing was destined to happen this way. Perhaps it was no accident he'd found Granger in the sutler's store and persuaded him to come along on this vacation on horseback. Maybe the trails of the scouts and the massive body of Indians had intersected at this island in the Arikaree to fulfill some kind of divine plan. Maybe. . . .

But no! He would not allow himself to think that way. A man couldn't go through life believing everything he did or everything that happened around him was foreordained. Some religions believed so, but it contradicted his own belief in the free will of human beings. There were many things a person couldn't control, yet he still had choices and men made those choices every day. A Supreme Being might know what those choices would lead to, but they were still free choices.

Thinking thus, he finally grew weary and, toward dawn, drifted into a doze. When he cracked his eyes, gray daylight was illuminating the besieged men barricaded in their trenches by dead horses and the breastworks of upended saddles and ridges of dirt.

The scouts stirred as dawn arrived. Sentries that Sergeant McCall had posted near the shoreline of the island were relieved and went to their blankets.

Talbot looked across at Granger who was rubbing his eyes and appearing more haggard than ever. The jokes and bravado seemed to have fallen away from his friend like a torn mask. The realization of their fate must be settling in as the third day of the siege began.

CHAPTER SEVEN

The third day started much as the second had ended. Indian sharpshooters took up positions on the hillsides and resumed sporadic firing. It was evident they weren't interested in pursuing the attack with the same vigor as before.

Forsyth passed the word through Sergeant McCall that the scouts would preserve their ammunition and not return fire unless an Indian carelessly exposed himself.

A little before noon, Jim Curry, one of the scouts, bored with inaction, said he intended to crawl to the head of the island through the tall grass and bushes to "see if maybe I can pick me off one o' them red bastards before lunch." With a loaded Spencer, he disappeared on hands and knees into the thick growth.

Ten minutes later surprised yells burst from the thicket, followed by a gunshot. Curry crashed back out of the bushes. "Injuns!"

Talbot grabbed his carbine. Several men sprang forward.

"Where?"

"There!" Curry pointed toward the slim cottonwood at the head of the island. "I was slippin' along through the grass and come nose to nose with an Injun sneakin' up on us."

"Heard a shot. Did ya get him?"

"No." Curry was wide-eyed. "But he didn't get me, either."

Several of the scouts chuckled. "I reckon that Indian is still running," Grover said, lowering the hammer on his Colt. The sound of laughter had been missing since the attacks started. It loosened the mood and seemed strangely restorative.

Forsyth called Grover to him and inquired about the commotion, then asked the chief scout if he thought the Indians had withdrawn, since the firing had now ceased. He glanced toward the surrounding hilltops where the families had their camps. "Even the women have stopped that incessant wailing."

"Don't reckon they're gone just yet, Major, but they might've pulled back some to regroup. Maybe mourn their dead. I'd guess they're likely having a council to decide what to do with us. They've paid a heavy price so far, and might think it wiser just to leave us stranded afoot with our wounded."

Major Forsyth nodded and, grimacing, shifted his position on the blanket.

Grover followed the major's gaze toward the apparently deserted hillsides. "Sir, I could take a few men and cross over to our old campsite to see if there's anything useful we might've left behind."

"Go ahead. Just be careful you don't get yourselves picked off by some sharpshooters."

The besieging Indians were nowhere in evidence. They'd drawn away, leaving the scouts on their sandbar surrounded by rotting horseflesh grilling in the last throes of the summer sun. In place of war whoops and gunshots, the only sounds to be heard were the soft gurgling of the shallow stream, the whispering of a prairie breeze in the tall grass, and the chirping of birds in the bushes. In a way, this return to the murmuring of Nature was more unnerving than actual battle — an eerie peace before another storm of lead, powder smoke, and death.

An hour later, Grover and five scouts returned with a coffee pot and a handful of spilled coffee beans. The men crushed the beans and gathered enough dry arrow shafts to kindle a small fire. The wounded men welcomed the weak coffee that was brewed for them.

In the more relaxed atmosphere, the men managed to kindle a larger, smoky fire with dead twigs and green brush. Several scouts prepared a stew composed of horse meat mixed with gunpowder, and handfuls of grass and herbs that appeared edible.

Talbot sipped the concoction from his tin cup. "Whose idea was this, anyway?"

"Some of the old-timers swear that black powder offsets the taste of rotting meat," Granger replied, taking a tentative bite of the stew. "Sort of like curry. Reckon it disguises the flavor some, but I don't know if it'll keep your insides from knowing the difference."

Talbot sat down next to his rifle pit. "They can starve us out. We can't go on like this much longer." He forced down another swallow of the stew. "If I didn't know better, I'd say they're gone."

"Peaceful silence," Granger agreed. "You'd think we could walk right out of here."

"Likely wouldn't get far," Talbot said, envisioning murderous savages ripping him apart with knives. He shook his head to blunt the overactive imagination, then glanced at the major several yards away. Forsyth was lolling back against a saddle, eyes closed. Talbot wondered if gangrene would set in if the commander's leg wounds were left untreated much longer.

He turned back to Granger. "You reckon those two couriers got through the other night?"

"Even if they did, it's over a hundred mile walk to Fort Wallace." He paused. "And just as far back, even mounted." His tone wasn't optimistic.

An hour later, Talbot was dozing in the shade when a shot broke the silence. The men jumped to their arms. In a few minutes, two scouts emerged from the deep grass holding a lean coyote by the hind leg. "Something for the cooking pot," one of them announced.

"Don't believe I'm quite that hungry, yet," Granger muttered under his breath.

The others were less squeamish and the animal was skinned, cooked, and added to the stew that was devoured with evident relish by the majority of the group.

Young Schlesinger took a bowl of stew to Major Forsyth.

"Smells pretty good," the commander

remarked, taking up the spoon to eat. "I don't want to know what's in it."

As evidence the Indians hadn't given up the fight, the tedious afternoon hours were broken four times by individual forays, three by braves on horseback, and one afoot. One of the attackers tumbled from his swift pony, struck by a carbine bullet. The experienced plainsmen were convinced the probes were not so much intended to kill scouts as to showcase the bravery and enhance the reputations of young, untested warriors.

Shortly thereafter, two mounted Indians appeared at a distance, splashing slowly downstream toward the head of the island. One was waving a carbine with a white rag attached to the barrel.

Forsyth studied them through his field glasses. "What do you make of that, Mister Grover?"

"I don't reckon they're a peace commission," the head scout replied. "More'n likely they want to parley for the body of that Injun shot off his horse a little while ago. And get up close where they can see what kinda shape we're in."

"Sergeant, tell the men to shoot the first Indian who comes within range," the major said.

A Spencer roared and the slug skipped off

the surface of the water a hundred feet short. The Indians halted, appeared to confer, then turned and rode slowly away.

Toward sunset, Forsyth told McCall to gather the able-bodied scouts around him. When they assembled, he said: "We're in a tight spot here. I don't know if the two men I sent out the other night got through, so I'm going to try again." He held up three pages torn from his memorandum book. "Here's the letter I'm sending with the couriers . . . 'On Delaware Creek, Arikaree River, September Nineteenth, Eighteen Sixty-Eight, to the Commanding Officer, Fort Wallace . . . I sent you two messengers on the night of the Seventeenth instant, informing you of my critical condition. I tried to send two more last night, but they did not succeed in passing the Indian pickets, and returned. If the others have not arrived, then hasten at once to my assistance. I have eight badly wounded and ten slightly wounded men to take in, and every animal I had was killed, save seven, which the Indians stampeded. Lieutenant Beecher is dead, and Acting Assistant-Surgeon Mooers probably cannot live the night out. He was hit in the head Thursday, and has spoken but one rational word since.

I am wounded in two places . . . in the right thigh and my left leg broken below the knee. The Cheyennes alone number four hundred and fifty or more. Mister Grover says they never fought so before. They are splendidly armed with Spencer and Henry rifles. We killed at least thirty-five of them, and wounded many more, besides killing and wounding a quantity of their stock. They carried off most of their killed during the night, but three of their men fell into our hands. I am on a little island, and have still plenty of ammunition left. We are living on horse meat, and are entirely out of rations. If it was not for so many wounded, I would come in, and take the chances of whipping them if attacked. They are evidently sick of their bargain. I had two of the members of my company killed on the Seventeenth . . . namely, William Wilson and George W. Chalmers. You had better start with not less than seventy-five men, and bring all the wagons and ambulances you can spare. Bring a six-pound howitzer with you. I can hold out here for six days longer if absolutely necessary, but please lose no time. Very respectfully, your obedient servant, George A. Forsyth, U.S. Army, Commanding Company Scouts. P.S. . . . My surgeon having been mortally wounded, none of my wounded have had their wounds dressed yet, so please bring out a surgeon with you.' " He looked up at the attentive faces around him. "I'm sending Donovan and Pliley with this note. Any questions or comments?"

The men turned grizzled, sunburned faces toward one another, but no one said a word.

"All right," Forsyth concluded, "these two men will leave at midnight."

Pliley and Donovan went about their preparations with a grave air, apparently knowing all eyes were on them. Talbot wondered if he was looking on these two for the last time. He doubted the other men were envious of the couriers' mission; there'd been no rush to volunteer.

The pair stuffed their pockets with strips of rotting meat. Then they exchanged their boots for moccasins taken from the bodies of dead Indians who'd fallen nearby.

The night turned cold and Talbot was still awake, shivering, in his rifle pit several hours later as the murky forms of Pliley and Donovan slipped quietly away.

Sometime before dawn Talbot awoke to a gusty wind. At first he thought a cold rain shower was passing over, but then felt snowflakes brushing his face. He pulled the blanket over his head and managed to doze off again.

Daylight revealed an inch of wet snow blanketing everything. The couriers had not returned and, in spite of the wet and chill, a hopeful air pervaded the little camp.

A dense fog rose from the warmer surface of the surrounding water, cutting off all sight and sound, and making the island seem even more isolated.

By mid-morning, the sun broke through the twisting tendrils of mist and began to burn away the icy fog. An hour later, everyone was basking in the warming sun while the snow was melting into slush and mud. Blankets and shirts were spread over bushes to dry, and several of the scouts were grousing about wanting a cup of coffee.

Some of the severely injured were feverish. Several of the healthy men bathed the faces of their helpless comrades and changed dressings on the wounds — about all they could do to soothe them.

Another batch of rotten meat stew flavored with gunpowder was cooked and consumed. Normally not a picky eater, Talbot couldn't get it past his nose. If he stayed here much longer, he'd be eating anything, even if it gave him food poisoning. But, for now, the misery of hunger was preferable to the misery of nausea and vomiting. He cinched up his belt a notch and lay down on his blanket to conserve energy.

As this fourth day began, an idea that'd been flitting on the fringes of his mind thrust itself to the fore — escape. It was too late to volunteer as a courier as a means of getting away. But it wasn't too late for him to slide out of this trap alone. His chances of making it past the surrounding Indians seemed much improved now that the besiegers had withdrawn. It was a certainty unseen Indian sentries still encircled the island. And, in the quiet of night, without the previous wailing of women to mask sounds of his going, would he be able to slip past them? He mulled over the possibilities for a time.

Many of the other men, probably including his closest friend, Phil Granger, would consider him a coward. If he were caught and killed trying to get away, they'd probably take the attitude it was only just punishment. But in that event, he'd be past caring. Living — not dying — was his goal. At age twenty-four, he'd just begun to experience the joy of living. Everything that could be done here had already been done. Now, all they could do was wait. Why should he sacrifice himself to some artificial code of honor by staying? Some warrior tribes, like the Apaches, had no such compunction about fleeing a fight, if chances of winning or survival were slim. It was considered the smart thing to do. This whole business of dying with honor was an archaic concept handed down from white European armies of the past.

The more he considered the idea of individual escape, the more reasonable it seemed. He made up his mind he wouldn't sit here and starve, even if others still held out hope for rescue — a vain hope, in his opinion. Once the decision was made, he began to lay plans. He would take his loaded Spencer and a canteen of water, along with his Colt, thirty rounds of ammunition, and his belt knife. There was no food fit to carry. His corduroy jacket, dirty and damp, his felt hat, and deerskin gloves would protect him from the elements once past the watchful eyes of the Indian sentries. That would be the tricky part. He'd need extreme care and luck. It was a desperate gamble. Unless he was killed outright, an agonizing death awaited him if caught by Indians. Death out there was a chance; death here was a certainty.

He lay on his blanket in the rifle pit, sipping from the canteen of water drawn from the shallow well nearby. Even though filtered through cotton cloth, it still tasted of dirt, but was cleaner than the stream itself, which contained dead animals and manure.

Yesterday, he'd gone to assist with the wounded, but found their close friends had already provided what little help could be given without a doctor. The sight of their suffering and the festering wounds were nearly more than he could bear. His sympathy for their suffering led him to the thought that he could wind up just like them, lingering in a horror-filled twilight of agony, awaiting the oblivion of death. What made it even worse, was that it was all so unnecessary. This was what humans did to one another intentionally, fighting over land.

Fatigue and depression went hand in hand. So he was determined to get what sleep he could. He stretched out and tilted his hat over his eyes. After a time, he slid into a doze. When he roused himself and yawned, he felt a bit more refreshed, although his stomach was growling. Even when he willed to ignore it, the gnawing of hunger was always there, just at the edge of his consciousness. It was definitely time for him to get away while he still had the strength.

He looked across at Granger whose face

had begun to disappear behind a scruffy reddish beard. His friend was chewing on a bone that had lately served a coyote as a rib. Talbot said nothing. He wondered why scouts didn't venture out to salvage meat from one or two of the dead Indian ponies that lay near the banks of the stream. Then he realized these animals had been shot down the first day of the battle and were at the same stage of decomposition as their own horses.

When Granger met his glance and grinned, Talbot dropped his gaze, wondering if Granger could read his thoughts by looking into his eyes. Talbot swallowed. He'd never been a good poker player; his face gave him away every time.

As he was looking down, the condition of his boots startled him. He'd have to do something about this footgear if he expected to walk upward of a hundred miles. The leather was soggy and his socks were wet inside — a perfect recipe for softened skin and raw feet. Not only that but the stitching was rotting and the soles were beginning to separate. These boots were two years old and had seen much hard use, mostly within the past few weeks. There was no time to dry them, and no means to repair them. He'd have to throw them away, and maybe rip up part of his shirt and wrap his feet in the cloth. Lack of usable footwear could doom his whole scheme. If he had to walk barefoot, he'd be crippled within three miles.

Talbot stood and pulled his Colt, checking to be sure it was fully loaded. "I'm going exploring," he announced to Granger, who was watching him curiously. "Just to kill some time and look around. Haven't seen anything but a few square yards of this island."

Without waiting for a reply, he plunged into the waist high grass, then crouched and slipped past a clump of bushes. The network of trenches was quickly lost to sight behind him. He was exploring, all right, but for a particular item. Just beyond the slim cottonwood near the head of the island, he found what he was looking for. A brown, bare leg protruded from a thicket a few feet ahead. Talbot drew his gun and crept forward to investigate. He holstered his weapon when the stench and the buzzing flies told him there was nothing to fear from this Indian.

The body lay face down, dressed only in a breechclout, a single eagle feather in his scalp lock. He'd fallen too near the scouts for his friends to retrieve the body. Talbot slipped off the dead man's moccasins, satisfied to see the heavy brush had sheltered them from the light snow. The rawhide was still dry. They were fairly new and the soles thick and stiff, while the uppers were soft and flexible. A pattern of three diamond-shaped porcupine quills dyed red and green decorated the tops. He didn't know, or care, what tribe this brave had belonged to as he held the moccasins to his own feet and grunted in satisfaction. Close enough to a fit, and he'd secure them to his ankles with the rawhide thongs to be sure. Sitting down, he tugged off his wet boots and socks, then massaged his wrinkled, wet feet, until they were dry and smooth and pink. He pulled on the dry, comfortable moccasins, tied the thongs around his ankles, and stood up. Perfect. If one believed in Providence, this had to be a good example of it.

He looked down at the dead Indian whose face was hidden in the grass. "You don't need these moccasins any more. But I do." Turning away, he wondered why all human situations couldn't dovetail as neatly as this.

CHAPTER EIGHT

Talbot could hardly see in the gathering darkness. The camp was taking longer than usual to settle down. It was probably his imagination, but men seemed to be moving around more, talking, digging, and tending the tiny cooking fire under the stew pot steaming the air with a nauseating odor. He'd never get used to the putrid decay of bloated, rotting flesh.

Four sentries vanished quietly to their posts — a pair to each side of the island. Try as he might to see their location, Talbot lost them in the murk. They stationed themselves somewhere in the brush along the shore. It wouldn't do to be shot by a nervous guard while trying to slide out of there.

Before lying down, he cut two strips from the edge of his blanket and tied them around his feet over the moccasins for additional padding and to keep from leaving identifiable tracks. His gun belt buckled in place and his hat beside him, he lay in his rifle pit, staring at the cloudless sky spangled with stars. He'd prayed for a murky overcast, but it was not to be. He couldn't wait another twenty-four hours in hopes of bad weather. Maybe God was setting him up for failure by making the night so bright, he thought, noting the rising moon. He chuckled at the idea that direct intervention by the Almighty would be required to frustrate his plan.

The scouts were often restless during the night, many unable to sleep for whatever reasons. Others muttered incoherently in their dreams, rolling over and over. It was the same this night. Granger stood up, blanket shrouding his shoulders, and moved off toward the latrine trenches dug twenty yards south of the last rifle pits. A few minutes later he returned and rolled into his trench with a groan to resume sleep.

The latrines! That was it — his way out without being noticed.

He waited impatiently until the moon had moved a good distance across the sky. He sensed it was after midnight. Granger's breathing was deep and regular, and most of the others were very likely asleep as well. Talbot knew that he'd never catch them all asleep at once; a few would always be awake. But it was time to go. He drew a deep breath, wrapping the blanket around his shoulders as if for warmth, but actually to hide his carbine and canteen. Crawling out of the pit, he hunched over and stepped with care between the trenches. The moonlight created sharp black shadows that hid him quickly when he ducked into the brush and followed the beaten track toward the latrines.

He was in luck. No one was at the latrines and he skirted the stinking trenches, moving quietly toward the lower end of the island. Every few moments, he stopped and held his breath, listening. From somewhere in the distance came the mournful howl of a coyote. He pushed aside the bushes, making more noise than intended.

Suddenly the loud click of a cocking rifle broke the stillness.

Talbot halted, heart pounding so loud in his ears, he could hear nothing else.

"You better answer me in good American, or I'm gonna cut loose," came a low voice somewhere to his right.

"Take it easy!" Talbot answered quickly, trying to keep his voice steady. "I was using the latrine and must've got turned around."

No answer for several seconds. He heard

someone move in the brush. "Trenches are back the way you come," the sentry's voice said.

"Thanks." Talbot moved away from the voice, purposely crashing through the thick brush. After a dozen steps — more than ten yards — he slowed, went to his hands and knees, and, orienting himself by the moon, crawled toward the end of the island. The Spencer carbine proved cumbersome in the heavy brush, and he considered abandoning it, but decided he might need it later.

His stomach growled so loudly he felt sure it could be heard several yards away. He began to regret not bringing along some of the rotting meat. By spitting a few strips of the softening horseflesh on a green stick and roasting it nearly black over the fire, he might have made it palatable. But it was too late for regrets. Now he was committed and there was no going back. The end of the island seemed a long way off. His pants legs grew soaked in the wet grass, and the exercise of crawling was all that kept him from becoming chilled.

Abruptly the bushes ended and Talbot stopped, panting softly, to gaze at the open vista of the river below the island. Listening intently, he heard nothing, save the barely discernible swish and gurgle of water over and around a dead snag whose grotesque upraised limbs stood out, stark and black, against the pale background of the sandy riverbed.

In the bright moonlight, he studied the terrain, a section at a time, wishing he had a pair of field glasses. He doubted any Indian sentries were afoot within view of the island. Although this possibility couldn't be discounted, it was far likelier these warriors of the plains would be patrolling on horseback.

Less than a quarter mile downstream, a shallow ravine opened on the right, probably worn into the bank by years of run-off. It was dry now in September and he'd use it to leave the riverbed.

His moccasins, and blanket strips binding them, were already damp, but he untied the strips and put them into his pocket. In the moonlit world of black and gray, he would stand out plainly to anyone watching, but it couldn't be helped. He folded the blanket, corner to corner and threw it over one shoulder, tucking the ends into his belt, fore and aft. Stepping boldly into the open, he gripped his Spencer and waded into the clear, shallow river. He walked cautiously downstream. The water was knee-deep and cold.

Before he'd gone fifty yards, the soft thudding of many hoofs caused his heart to skip a beat. He splashed toward the big dead snag as his only cover. Moments later, a party of Indians rode into view around a bend on the hard sand. The thick cottonwood trunk lay on its side, barkless and silver in the moonlight, it's remaining limbs angling upward in mute supplication against final dissolution. The imbedded snag was all that stood between him and the approaching war party. He was close enough that he sank slowly to his knees in several inches of water and crawled the last few feet to flatten his body against the thickest of its upraised limbs, hardly daring to breathe. He willed to become one with the dead tree.

They passed on, riding slowly, not talking and apparently not seeing his motionless form in dark clothes, hugging the crooked snag.

When they were at a safe distance, he started again, determined to escape the sandy riverbed the Indians were apparently using for a moonlit road. He moved, hunched over like some night animal until he reached and faded into the inky shadow of the ravine. Following the ravine a quarter mile until it rose and flattened, he came out onto a long, open slope, covered with patches of prickly pear. One hand, his lower pants legs, and the tops of his moccasins were filled with the thin quills before he realized it, and he stood up, cursing softly at the stabbing pain. There was enough moonlight that he could identify the scattered patches and he quickly moved on, avoiding the cactus, and ignoring the imbedded cactus spines for now. He was in full view on the open plain, but he could also see anyone else at a distance. And he did. Twice in the next hour he changed direction to avoid roaming parties of Indians on horseback. There were a lot of night patrols out, he thought, or else they'd somehow discovered sign of his exit from the island and were looking for him.

He sat on the ground and retied the blanket strips around his feet to further pad the moccasins that, although sturdy and well made, had softened in the water and were not designed for long-distance walking.

By the time the moon set and pre-dawn darkness enveloped him, he felt safer. *Blacker than sin and death,* he mused to himself, pausing to catch his breath and try to get his bearings by way of the North Star. Then he hunkered down for a long minute to ease his leg and back muscles and extract as many prickly pear quills as possible before moving on.

Before he realized it, he could make out details distinctly; dawn was coming. He began to look for a daytime hiding place, estimating he was probably no more than four miles from the island due to his late start and having to avoid the war parties. Adrenaline flow had forestalled fatigue, but now that he was beyond imminent danger, he was beginning to droop.

Just as the fiery orb of sun tipped the eastern horizon, he spotted something moving far off on the plains. Antelope herd or marauding Indians, he couldn't tell which, but he kept trudging southward, looking for a hiding place, and finding none.

The moving figures slowly grew more distinct as the distance lessened and the light increased. He hunkered to rest and narrowed his eyelids to focus better. He'd swear it was Indians. But he couldn't stop here long to find out. In a low swale of ground just ahead lay the head and horns of a long dead buffalo. Besides the skull, all that remained of the animal was remnants of rotted furry hide draped over the partly exposed rib cage and pelvis. Nature was gradually reclaiming its own as the carcass settled back into the earth. Two leg bones were disarticulated as if dragged a few yards away by wolves or coyotes. If this big bull had died of natural causes, the vultures and other scavengers would have disposed of all edible parts within a few days. He squatted to inspect it as a possible hiding place. Only a musty smell remained. For lack of a better choice, this would have to do for shelter today.

He poked his carbine barrel inside the natural tent to rake out dead grass and any insects. Sudden movement and a dry buzzing made him jump back, heart racing. A rattlesnake had thrown itself into a coil, diamond-shaped head poised to strike. The thick-bodied serpent had lain perfectly camouflaged in the dead grass.

Talbot let out a long breath. *Good thing I didn't put my hand in there,* he thought, retreating still farther. He looked up and saw the Indians closing the distance, horses loping. He had to get that damned snake out of there so he could hide. Which would be worse — venom injected into an arm vein, or being caught and tortured by those approaching Indians.

Leaning away as far as possible, he thrust his Spencer barrel toward the snake. The rattler struck with blurring speed. Startled, Talbot dropped the weapon, and crept back

130

a few yards, staying low behind the remains of the carcass. The snake, apparently sensing a chance to escape the trap, dropped out of its coil and slithered swiftly through the rib cage, and was gone. Talbot heard the sibilant sound of its going, then nothing. The breeze whispered through the tall grass across the warming prairie.

He retrieved the Spencer and raked it around inside the hollow to be sure there were no more hazards before he crawled inside. Positioning himself on one elbow, he could see out below a flap of hanging hide. If he remained still, his brown clothing would blend well with the buffalo hide. Because of a low vantage point, his distance view was restricted by the gentle swell of ground.

He finally tired of waiting for the riders to appear and lay back, using his crushed hat for padding under his head. Once he stretched out, his weary body was ready to relax into sleep, in spite of his resolve to stay alert until the danger passed. He snorted with the beginnings of a snore and woke himself. He peered out, but nothing was within his purview. Maybe the riders had turned from their course and gone in another direction.

When he again jerked awake, the sun was

higher, and baking him through several holes in the tattered hide. The sound of voices made his heart leap. Except for his eyes, he dared not move. He could see nothing from his angle of repose, but could still hear voices in a conversational tone, rising and falling. They were close enough that he knew they weren't speaking English.

There was no urgency to their voices, so he assumed they hadn't seen him. They sounded close and weren't moving. But why had they stopped here? If they'd been riding all night, maybe they were preparing to camp. Panic gripped his stomach. He'd seen no stream nearby, so they hadn't paused to water their horses. He chanced turning his head ever so slightly in that direction. He could just make out four feathered heads above the edge of the buffalo shoulder bone. They were less than thirty yards away. The heat of the sun, his windless shelter, and the proximity of the hostiles made sweat trickle down his face and sides. As the minutes dragged on, he began to itch, first in the small of his back, then behind his ear, then in eight or ten more places all over his body. He dared not move to scratch. Was his clothing infested with lice? He'd never had them before and didn't know how they felt. Probably just dirt and sweat and nerves were combining to cause this exquisite agony. Sweat coursed down his face into his ears and the creases of his neck. He gritted his teeth and suffered the tortures of the damned.

The pungent aroma of tobacco smoke drifted to his nostrils on the light breeze. They'd stopped to smoke and stretch. He remained motionless, trying to blend in with the hollow, woolly carcass as if he were part of the ground.

At long last, he heard a low laugh and then soft thudding of hoofs moving closer. He tensed, his hand sliding to his holstered Colt. When they walked their horses near and those keen eyes spotted him, he'd have the advantage of surprise. Even if they had firearms, and his hand wasn't shaking too badly, he could get one or two before they got him.

They rode within ten feet, and one of the ponies tossed its head and whinnied as they passed, walling its eyes at the dead buffalo and its human cargo.

The Indian rider savagely jerked the animal's head back forward with a sharp word and the riders disappeared over a swell of grassy ground. Within a minute they were out of earshot. Only then did he relax and begin to scratch the dozen itchy spots.

The rest of the day he slept undisturbed, awaking hungry and thirsty in late afternoon. Several swallows of his canteen water only served to stimulate his gastric juices. He nearly doubled over from sharp hunger pangs. If the Indians hadn't been so close, he could've shot the fat rattler for food. But, as long as he was wishing, he thought, crawling outside and cinching his belt up a notch, he might as well wish himself safe and full and comfortable somewhere in a civilized town miles away from here.

Creeping up the lip of the swale, he scanned the prairie in all directions without skylighting himself. Empty. Waiting for full darkness, he spent the rest of daylight picking the remaining cactus spines from his hand and the tops of his moccasins caused by his crawl through the prickly pear.

Then he hefted his Spencer, looped the canteen over the other shoulder, and set off walking south, reveling in the comfort of dry moccasins and, in spite of feeling weak from hunger, satisfied that things were beginning to go his way. Only once, during that long night hike, did he see riders in the far moonlight; he lay flat on the ground until they passed without coming closer, like a ship moving at an oblique angle across the horizon.

With the coming of darkness also came a cold wind from the northwest that blew at his back, giving him an extra push. To take advantage of it, and to stay warm, he alternately jogged and walked. A cover of clouds blew over, obscuring moon and stars, and he had a bit of trouble orienting himself in moving directly south.

In the gray light of dawn, he located a hollow rimmed with the leaves and stalks of dead sunflowers. After cautiously making sure no animals had taken shelter there, he bedded down for the day, dry and warm out of the wind, but considerably weaker from lack of food. Only two or three small swallows remained in his canteen; he'd have to find water. The hollow where he lay ran eastward, deepening into a narrow cut and then widening. Probably another gully eroded by run-off into a stream. He'd follow it tonight.

Five hours of sleep proved enough to restore his energy — or at least what energy remained in his weakened body. From the position of the sun, it was only about noon, but he was impatient to set out, even in full daylight. By staying in the narrow gully, he remained hidden as he worked his way down until the gully broadened and he could walk easily in the bottom strewn with small stones and mud. He didn't care whether he left tracks. He was either getting careless, or confident in his ability to avoid hostile Indians. The wash extended a mile before it finally joined a stream the size of the river where the scouts were besieged. He stooped to fill his canteen from the clear water flowing over a gravel bar and wondered if this might, in fact, be the same stream. Based on the direction he'd been traveling, he doubted it.

He carefully rinsed out his bandanna and strained the water through it. This precaution likely wouldn't prevent any sickness should the water be poisoned by anything like a dead animal upstream. He only knew his mother had instilled her obsessive habit of cleanliness in him. He took a long drink, then strained more water to refill the canteen. If he reached civilization alive, he resolved to visit his mother. She'd moved to St. Louis from Baltimore two years earlier, and was working as a domestic there.

For an hour he rested by the stream, listening to the soothing wind rushing through the tops of the big cottonwood trees. Then he retreated back up the dry wash to the level of the prairie above.

Suddenly he heard a strange bleating noise and stiffened to attention. He crouched in the tall grass like some hunted animal. A chill went over him as the sound grew closer. He gripped the Spencer and looked up. A flock of honking geese was flying southward in a ragged V-formation. A relieved sigh whooshed from his lungs as he stood up, lowering the hammer on his carbine. He was not only weak, but his nerves also quivered on edge.

He took his bearings by the westering sun and started south again, wishing he could make the speed of the vanishing geese. As he neared Fort Wallace, he veered slightly west. If he encountered any soldiers, he'd send them to the relief of the scouts.

The sun set and the night came on clear and windless, a chill of approaching autumn in the air. Now toughened to foot travel, he moved steadily, swinging along at an easy gait of five or six miles an hour.

When dawn came, he felt safe enough to keep moving by daylight now that he was at least sixty miles from the island. So far, he had not tried to hunt, even though at dawn the previous day he'd come across a prairie-dog town. The elusive animals had vanished into their burrows at his approach. It mattered not, since he still couldn't risk firing a shot that could be heard a long distance.

Shortly after noon, he stumbled upon a

137

rutted, dusty road running northeast to southwest. Its sudden appearance surprised him. Evidently well traveled, the road might connect the string of forts across Kansas. He had only a vague idea where he was; he could even be west of Kansas. As long as it afforded easier walking for his weakening legs, he didn't really care where the road led. He turned to follow it westward. The lack of food was beginning to tell now and he tired easily. If he got into a rhythm of walking, he could continue for miles. But once he stopped and sat down, he could hardly get up again.

By late afternoon, weakness and the long hours of walking finally forced him to seek rest at the side of the empty road. He'd seen no one all day, and was startled when a sudden rumble of hoofs and wheels jerked up his attention. A westbound stage was coming. He jumped up and waved his arm, silhouetting himself against the red glow of the western sky.

"*Whoa! Whoa,* there!" The driver drew the galloping six-horse hitch to a halt, the trailing dust cloud catching up and swirling around the Concord coach.

"What's your next stop?" Talbot called.

"Cheyenne Wells," the driver replied. "Two dollar fare."

Talbot didn't really care where the next stop was as long as he didn't have to walk any more. Luckily he still had most of his pay from his last scouting job, and handed up a quarter eagle. "Keep the change." He noted the shotgun guard eyeing him, and was suddenly aware the man was staring at his dust-covered moccasins.

"You're a long way from anywhere, mister," the guard remarked, resting his double-barrel coach gun across his left arm.

"Horse stepped in a prairie dog hole thirty miles north," Talbot explained, reaching for the door handle. "Had to shoot him." Yanking open the door, he pulled himself up inside and flopped wearily into a leather-covered seat as the coach lurched into motion and the door swung shut.

He was bone-weary, but thank God he'd made it! He leaned his Spencer into a corner before he looked up and realized he had company.

CHAPTER NINE

A middle-aged, graying man sat opposite him, the only other passenger in the stage. Well dressed in whipcord pants, shiny black boots, Tattersall check vest, white shirt, and string tie, he'd doffed his coat and hat and placed them on the seat beside him.

The man nodded and smiled.

"Howdy," Talbot muttered, hardly aware of anything but his overpowering fatigue. Never, in his twenty-four years, had he been so exhausted. A naked woman would have elicited no interest from him. He leaned into the corner and closed his eyes.

"Care for a drink?" A sonorous voice penetrated his fogged brain.

Talbot opened his eyes, and tried to focus.

"If you don't mind my saying so, you look hard used. Maybe something to brace you up?" The man held out a silver pocket flask.

Talbot hesitated, recalling the pledge he'd taken in his early teens against the use of hard liquor. "Taking the Pledge" was common among many of the Irish who were prone to overindulge. His late father had been a slave to "demon rum" as the pious reformers called it.

Surely his circumstance called for an exception to this pledge. If he didn't get something besides water into his stomach, he felt his body and soul stood a good chance of parting company before the stage reached Cheyenne Wells. Feeling relatively safe in the coach, he had a further letdown of his determined energy. The life force was draining out of him like water from an unplugged bathtub.

He reached for the flask. "Thanks." He turned it up and took two swallows. The fiery brandy hit the back of his throat, causing a reflexive cough, tears blurring his vision. The liquor burned a path to his stomach. He gasped, let it settle, and took two more small swallows. He handed the flask back while the brandy silently exploded in his empty stomach, spreading a warm glow that radiated through his insides. Within a minute, he felt strength and energy flowing back into his limbs. Surely this was a heaven-sent angel of mercy providing him a reprieve from death.

The stranger slid the flask into an inside

pocket of his coat lying on the seat.

Talbot inhaled a deep breath and sat up straight. He felt obliged to introduce himself. "Matthew Talbot," he said, giving his real name before he had time to think. He extended a hand.

"Norman Whitley," the gray-haired man replied.

"Thanks for the drink. What I really need is food. I haven't eaten in three or four days."

"You say your horse broke a leg thirty miles north?"

"*Uh* . . . yeah. Might've been farther. Don't rightly know." He had to be careful of being caught in a lie. It would've taken a healthy man only a day to walk to where the stage picked him up. And he was obviously suffering from exposure and hunger for longer than one day.

But Whitley merely nodded, not pressing for more. "In this country, a man afoot is often a man dead. Too much space, too many Indians."

For a minute, both men sat silently, Talbot reading the curiosity in Whitley's blue eyes.

Under normal circumstances, Talbot would have been mortified at his own appearance, especially in comparison to the man who sat opposite him. He cast his gaze downward at his muddy, stained pants and moccasins. He'd long since worn out and cast away the strips of blanket he'd tied around his feet. The remnant of the blanket was still rolled and slung on one shoulder. He rubbed a hand over the two-week growth of whiskers that furred his lean cheeks. His belt and holster hung loosely from his waist, the belt at the last notch. He'd been wearing these same clothes for more than two weeks now, and smelled of wood smoke, dried sweat, and unwashed body. Even to his own nose, he was giving off a miasma of mud, mold, and a variety of other unpleasant odors. He felt Whitley's eyes on him and decided to redirect the man's silent speculations.

"How far to Cheyenne Wells?"

"About fifteen miles."

"Is that all?"

"Right at it. Heard that driver charge you two dollars."

"I gave him two and a half."

"He's not above taking a little profit for himself. About three times what the fare ought to be."

"Maybe so, but I couldn't have walked another step."

"Those look like Cheyenne moccasins

you're wearing."

Talbot shrugged. "Don't know. Got 'em from a trader."

Another stretch of silence as the coach lumbered along at the pace of the trotting team, eating up the miles.

"What line of work you in?"

Whitley had violated the unwritten code of never prying into a man's personal business, unless information was first offered. But Talbot read it as an attempt at being sociable to pass the time.

"Mostly odd jobs. Work as a printer when I get a chance." He'd hardly passed the apprentice stage, but liked to think he could hold his own at job printing where speed was not as much a factor as in most newspaper offices.

"Well, you won't find any chance for a job like that in Cheyenne Wells. It's only a stage stop where there happens to be a spring." A smile creased the smooth-shaved cheeks.

"Where's the next town I can buy a horse?"

Whitley seemed to reflect a moment. "I reckon that'd be Denver. That's where I'm bound."

"How far?"

"Roughly a hundred thirty miles from Cheyenne Wells."

"Oh." Talbot began to wonder if he could make it that far. He didn't want to dig into his pockets to check his remaining finances in front of Whitley. That distance would mean about another day or so, counting stops. He could sleep in the coach and his stage fare included whatever poor food the swing stations provided. He began to feel he'd survive and find anonymity far from the ongoing disaster of the besieged scouts. He wondered if their situation had deteriorated since he left. It must have. Even if the massed warriors had not attacked again, the men must be starving, some of the more severely wounded probably dead by now. He thought of his friend Phil Granger, and had a sudden flush of guilt for abandoning him. He could feel his face reddening at the memory of sneaking away like a thief in the night, leaving Granger to his fate. Yet . . . there was nothing he could have done to help Granger or any of the others, a voice within him argued. He was only obeying nature's law of self-preservation. *Greater love than this, no man has, that he lay down his life for his friends.* The Biblical quote sprang to mind, unbidden. As true as that might be, why would a man throw away his own life, if it would not help others? The most he could have provided on that island was moral support, since all of them were sure to die within a few days, anyway.

The brandy began to affect him, and he couldn't hold his eyes open. He was grateful for the fatigue that began blurring his thinking.

"Hey, mister, this here's Cheyenne Wells."

Talbot came out of a drugged sleep and rubbed his eyes, blinking at the driver who was leaning in the stage door, shaking him. "If you're going on, I'll have to collect more fare."

"I reckon that quarter eagle I gave you will take me at least another thirty miles."

Norman Whitley, who'd stepped out of the stage on the other side, nodded. "That's right. And maybe even farther."

"This is none o' your affair!" the driver snapped.

"Don't let him buffalo you," Whitley said to Talbot.

The driver straightened up and glared at Whitley as if sizing up the man's resolve or ability with a gun. Apparently he decided not to chance it. "All right, this stage is headed to Denver. I'll haul you as far as Wild Horse. After that, it's more fare, or you're off." His belligerent expression softened when Talbot casually swung the barrel of the Spencer in his direction. "If you want to take a bath in that pond yonder, go ahead," the driver added in a milder tone.

"You saying I stink?" The brandy was making him arrogant.

"Might pick up a lady passenger or two along the way, is all," the driver said. "You got time. We'll be here an hour for supper and a change of horses." He stalked away toward the sod stage station.

Talbot headed for the pool formed by the spring's overflow. The edges of the small pond were thickly grown with willows. He pulled off his clothes and waded in, bare feet sinking into the soft mud bottom, then caught his breath as the cold water reached his groin. He wished he could also wash his clothes, but settled for scrubbing his skin until it tingled. He raked his scalp with his nails just in case of any vermin. The clothes would have to wait. He still had $11 in his pocket, and would need it until he could get a job. Denver seemed a likely place to lose himself and possibly find work as a printer. He'd heard the ten-year-old mining town had a transient population. One more drifter would never be noticed.

Fifteen minutes later he entered the stage station, wet hair plastered to his forehead under his hat.

Tough chunks of antelope steak in gravy served with cornbread constituted the meal. Talbot had to hold himself back from bolting the food and refilling his bowl. After his long fast, his stomach had shrunk, and too much food too quickly would likely make him sick.

"Ain't much, but it'll stick to your ribs," Whitley said under his breath, wiping his mouth with a bandanna he brought out of a pocket.

"I've never tasted anything better," Talbot answered truthfully, recalling all the fancier meals he'd eaten, but never appreciated. This was a feast to top any others. While he chewed and held his hunger in check, he felt Whitley eyeing him from across the table with more than casual interest. He didn't care. He'd find a job in Denver and scrape by until he could buy a $10 horse and $5 saddle. Time for him to quit doing odd jobs and get on with perfecting his newly acquired skill as a typesetter and printer.

He craved rest, and hoped he could at least partially recover from his ordeal by the time the coach reached Denver the following afternoon.

For the next ten hours, he slumped in a corner of the coach, Spencer propped beside him, his body accommodating itself to the pitch and sway of the tall Concord. Twice during the long night hours he was vaguely aware of stops at swing stations, men talking, a flash of lantern light at the windows. But he never fully woke.

Sometime later, he opened his eyes in response to the sound of his own name. "Huh?" He dragged himself out of deep sleep, rubbing his gritty eyes that were nearly stuck shut.

"Breakfast stop," Whitley said. "Better get something to eat."

"Breakfast?" He stumbled out of the coach, blinking at the clear sky beginning to lighten in the east. He breathed deeply of the cold, high plains air, feeling worse than he had the night before.

The older man walked inside with him, and the two sat down at a small wooden table where the smell of fried fatback made Talbot's stomach cringe. Feeling a bit shaky, he reached for the coffee pot.

Whitley's blue eyes regarded him "Reckon you're not a drinking man. That brandy hit you pretty hard." He reached for a small loaf of bread and tore off a chunk. "Well, I felt damned good for a while last night," Talbot admitted, sipping the scalding black coffee from a tin cup.

Sizzling fatback, curled up at the edges, was served up by the bearded stationkeeper. Talbot kept his stomach under control by concentrating on the sounds of the hostler changing teams outside the open door. Hell, if he could eat rotten horse stew, flavored with grass and gunpowder, he could surely keep this down. He'd seen other men hung over, and assumed he was experiencing a mild case of the same thing. Why did so many men crave alcohol if it made them feel like this? He didn't even feel rested after his sleep in the coach.

But he managed to eat two or three bites of the smelly pork and finished up with a big chunk of fresh bread and two more cups of coffee.

He urinated in the semi-darkness behind the log station before climbing back aboard the stage. As the miles rolled away behind them, taking him farther and farther from the scene of the siege, he began to feel better. As Whitley predicted, even his stomach and head gradually returned to normal.

Except for a little small talk about the weather, he stayed mostly to himself. He and Whitley remained the only passengers on this long, lonely stretch of road. But Talbot had an easy, outgoing nature and was afraid he'd tell more of himself than intended if he engaged in conversation.

He'd paid the new driver nine of his remaining $11 for the rest of his fare and food to Denver. How would he make it on $2 until the first payday of a job he didn't yet have? He thrust the worry from his mind. Something would turn up; it always did. If need be, he'd trade the Spencer.

The sun climbed higher overhead and then began a slide toward the barrier of mountains looming larger in the distance.

Finally, in late afternoon, the stage rolled up the dusty street and stopped at the stage depot. The two men alighted. Norman Whitley caught his leather valise the driver tossed down to him.

Talbot paused in the wan sunshine, looking down the street at the row of brick and frame buildings and a variety of store signs. He wondered what to do next.

"Well, Talbot, good luck to you. Maybe we'll run into each other. Denver's growing, but it's not that big," Whitley said, sounding weary. He thrust out a hand.

Talbot gripped it. "Thanks for your company . . . and the brandy. It likely saved my life."

Whitley chuckled. "You'd have survived without it. You're young. It's old men like me who need a boost from that stuff." He started to turn away, then swung around. "Here. . . ." He held out a coin.

Talbot could feel his face reddening. "Mister Whitley, I'm not a beggar. I can't take your charity."

"It's a loan. You can pay me back sometime."

"Not likely we'll meet again."

"Wish you'd humor me. There was a time, not long ago, when I didn't know where my next meal was coming from. And I benefited from the largesse of a total stranger. If it'll make you feel better, I sold some mining stock and I'm flush just now."

Talbot hesitated, knowing how much he could use the double eagle the man held between his fingers, out of view of the guard and driver and several other passengers waiting to board. He reached for the coin. It glowed in the last rays of the sun that rested atop the gray, wrinkled mountain range. "Thank you."

Whitley touched the brim of his hat and quickly moved away down the street.

Talbot found the nearest hotel that looked to be in his price range. He rented a room for a week, including the use of a tin bathtub. He bathed, then hurried out to a dry-goods store, whose sign was thrust out over the street. He replaced all his clothing, including underwear, socks, and boots. He tried them on in a dressing room and wore them out of the store with his old clothes wrapped in brown paper. Passing an alleyway, he dropped the bundle into a trash barrel, keeping only the moccasins. Why he kept them, he didn't rightly know. Instinct, perhaps? Maybe it was his only reminder of the sure death he'd escaped. But his Army Colt and Spencer would serve the same purpose, if he needed reminding. He doubted the memory would ever leave him.

As he opened the door to his hotel lobby, he wondered if Whitley would have been so generous if he'd known the real story. No sense torturing himself about that now. A good night's sleep and a good breakfast would put a better light on things when he went to find a job.

"Dammit, Talbot!" Big Bob Murphy exploded, dropping the proof sheet on the composing stone. "Eight errors in three paragraphs!" He stroked his thick beard with one hand and jabbed a finger at the heavily penciled sheet. "You're causing everyone a lot of extra time and work." He sounded more exasperated than angry. "I hired you because you assured me you were a typesetter. Reset that and be quick about it. You're throwing the whole production schedule off." He turned away and started for his office, then paused and swung around. "Maybe you're rusty 'cause you haven't worked for a while. So I'll give you three days to get yourself together and cut out those mistakes." He fixed Talbot with a forefinger. "But, if things haven't improved after that. . . ." He left the threat hanging and slammed the office door behind him.

Talbot's stomach contracted. He glanced around to see if anyone in the pressroom had observed the public reprimand. One of the printers was locking a page of type into the frame and gave no notice. The copy boy was scrubbing dirty type in a pan of solvent. Another man was adjusting the platen on the old Washington press. He nodded in the direction of the departed managing editor. "Don't let Murph get you down," he said in a low voice. "He's pretty rough around the edges sometimes, but he'll forget he said it five minutes from now. Something else will have him aggravated. Just fix it and go on. That's what the rest of us do. Murph's like a boiler. If he doesn't blow off steam now and again, he'd explode and kill us all." The man grinned, wiped a hand on his greasy pants leg, and held it out to shake. "Greg Stein. I've been on *The Gazette* two years,

154

so I've nearly got seniority around here."

"Matt Talbot." They shook. "Didn't he run off the last compositor?"

"Is that what he told you?" He chuckled. "Naw, Sam King just hates cold and snow. He went home to south Texas for the winter. He'll be back in the spring."

"I see." He propped the proof sheet where he could see the typos marked by an angry red pencil, picked up his composing stick, and began selecting type from the bins in front of him.

"Meek and humble . . . that's the way to act around Murph. Likes to be treated as the king," Stein continued. "When he starts stroking that damned beard, back off. That's a sure sign he's really riled. Reckon if he didn't have all that hair, his face'd be rubbed raw." He returned to his work. "There! Got that platen to slide slick as you please." He cast a glance toward the editor's closed door. "We'll have this edition put to bed in two hours. Want to join me for a drink? I'll be needing one by then."

"Sure." Talbot spoke before he recalled how rotten he'd felt from the hangover after drinking Whitley's brandy on an empty stomach. He'd watch himself this time. But he'd go to the saloon next door with Stein. After three days on the job, he was still a stranger in town and needed a friend.

Talbot liked the taste of the light, tangy draft brew and was into his third pint almost before he realized it. Stein was also a beer drinker, an easy man to talk to. Some years older than Talbot, the man didn't pry, seemed to take others at face value, and gave everyone the benefit of the doubt. Nevertheless, Talbot found himself embellishing his own background, either to protect his identity, or to make himself sound as if he'd led a more interesting life to this point. He told Stein he'd grown up in St. Louis, had always loved to read and determined early on to become a typesetter someday. Most of this was true. But he said both parents were dead, and, once he'd perfected his craft on small town papers, he planned to move back East to work for one of the big dailies, or possibly *Harper's Weekly* or *Leslie's Illustrated*. Even *The Atlantic Monthly* in upper crust old Boston wasn't beyond his ambition. His tongue seemed to be getting away from him as his confidence grew.

"Wish you luck. Myself, I've always been good with machinery, so I reckon I'm locked into what I do best."

More men crowded into the Union Saloon, dressed in canvas pants, woolen shirts, heavy vests, and jackets. Fresh from the loading docks, they carried the scent of mules and freshly cut lumber and a dozen other mixed odors. He overheard enough snatches of conversation about color and pokes of gold dust to surmise that the crusted mud he noticed on pants and boots had come from sluices, the chapped hands from raking pebbles out of cold creek water. The air around him was filled with loud talk, laughter, pipe smoke, and whiskey fumes.

They reminded Talbot, somewhat painfully, of the company of scouts he'd left behind to die on the island.

Stein seemed comfortable among these men, although Talbot suspected the older man was a mental cut above most of the workingmen in this place. Stein was either better schooled or better read. In the short time Talbot had worked at the paper, he noticed the lean, muscular pressman had a flair for things literary. Often, when the boss wasn't around, Stein would burst into snatches of song, usually some ribald ditty Or, out of the blue, would strike a dramatic pose and declaim the first three stanzas of some obscure poem. He kept the atmosphere loose and relaxed, and never seemed to take anything too seriously. "No need to get in a dither about that," was his favorite saying. "Leave it alone and it'll change by tomorrow."

Talbot had a good time, drank two or three more beers than he'd intended, but went home to his hotel about midnight feeling much better about himself and things in general than when he'd left work that day.

For the next four days, he took more time and care with his composing, and made only two errors. With steady practice, he grew adroit, and gradually picked up speed. Murphy slowed down his cursing and threatening. What eruptions did come from the managing editor were directed toward other people, and more often at Denver's rival newspapers.

Talbot collected his pay at the end of the week, breathing a sigh of relief at being slightly more financially secure. The $20 Whitley had given him had been the difference between having just enough, and begging, or borrowing.

Ten more days passed and he began to feel accepted as a quieter, more serious member of the *Gazette* staff. He became familiar with the handwriting of the various reporters, and with Murphy's corrections and marginal notes.

While setting type, he was only vaguely aware of the sense of what he composed. To get the gist of the piece, he usually glanced over the first paragraph or at the editor's penciled head before he began work.

On Thursday, the third week of October, sixteen days after he'd begun his job, he came in and started his usual routine. He picked up a page of copy Murphy had headed *DRAMATIC RESCUE.* Beneath those block letters were the words: *Several killed and wounded by hostile Indians during nine-day siege.*

Talbot's heart began to beat faster and his eyes skipped down the page, scanning the article. A column of cavalry had ridden to the relief of Colonel George Forsyth and his company of fifty civilian scouts. A cavalry patrol encountered two half-starved men on foot who'd escaped a tiny island in the Arikaree River. The piece went on to detail in words what Talbot knew by hard experience. His mouth grew dry and his throat tight as he read. He had no regrets about escaping alone. What he feared was the reaction of others.

The company of scouts was attacked by a combined force of at least 5,000 Sioux, Cheyenne, and Arapahoe warriors. During the battle, Roman Nose, feared Cheyenne chief, was killed. Among the scouts killed were Lt. Fred Beecher, and contract Surgeon Mooers. Several others were gravely wounded, including the commanding officer, Col. Forsyth, who suffered three gunshot wounds — one to each leg and one to the head. Although so severely injured that his wounds were infected and the doctors had to remove a piece of his skull bone, Lt. Col. Carpenter, who headed the 10th U.S. Cavalry relief column, found Col. Forsyth reclining in his trench, reading a copy of Oliver Twist.

While coolly holding off repeated mounted attacks from the brushy cover of a tiny island in the shallow river, the disciplined plainsmen, armed with Spencers and Colts, took a staggering toll of the savages. All of the scouts' mounts were killed, and the men survived on rotting horse meat and river water for the duration of the nine-day siege. By the time the relief column arrived, the Indians had withdrawn, but the survivors' condition was deplorable.

"My men all behaved honorably and fought bravely, even when the odds appeared to be overwhelming. Even two young men in their teens showed unusually courage under fire," Forsyth stated.

Sgt. McCall elaborated on the basic information supplied by the reticent colonel. "Colonel

Forsyth called us together on the 6th day of the siege when the Indians had apparently withdrawn. We were afoot and starving, and had almost no hope of survival. The colonel said anyone who wanted to leave and try to save himself was welcome to do so, since our chances were mighty slim. To a man, they vowed to stay with their wounded comrades and commander. All but one — a cowardly fella named Matt Talbot who skinned out a couple nights earlier.

He put down the paper and swallowed hard. His eyes were drawn back to the account.

"Do you know if this Talbot escaped to safety?"

"We don't know. The Indians might have got him," Sgt. McCall told this reporter.

The survivors of Forsyth's scouts have already begun calling the little isolated island in the river Beecher's Island, in honor of their officer killed there.

Talbot set the piece in type exactly as written. He never imagined he'd see himself called a coward in print — in print that he himself set.

When he finished his work for the day, he left in a daze and made for the Union Saloon. Would anyone even care if he'd slid away from Beecher's Island early? He'd only come to the same conclusion that Colonel Forsyth had when the commander, two days later, gave all the remaining scouts the chance to depart freely with no stigma.

Over his first two beers, he decided to forget the whole matter. Anybody who read the piece would never connect him with the Matt Talbot named by McCall.

This Western society was not class-conscious. A man's past was his own. Every man here had his own concerns, trying to wrest a living out of this new land. They had all they could do to take care of their own business — had no time or inclination to worry about somebody else's alleged cowardice. In his own mind, Talbot knew he'd acted logically, and obeyed nature's command for self-preservation. But that's not the way others would see it.

Even if someone identified and tried to give him a bad name, it would all be forgotten as soon as the next scandal hit the news. That's why newspapers continued to exist and sell — an unbroken series of sensational events.

That night he got drunk without intending to, and vomited on the street as he reeled toward his hotel at 2:00 in the morning.

The next day, Stein came looking for him

and rousted him out of bed. He soused Talbot's head under a pitcher of water, helped him into a clean shirt, and escorted him to the newspaper office two hours late. As bad as his head and stomach felt, Talbot was aware of the fact that his new friend, Stein, was uncharacteristically quiet and serious as they strode to the *Gazette* building. "The old man already got word you were out drunk last night," Stein said, gripping his arm and thrusting him along the dusty street. "So, whatever he says, just be humble and you'll keep your job."

Talbot caught his toe on the step up to the boardwalk.

"It's not like Murphy doesn't have a taste for John Barleycorn himself," Stein said. "But he never lets it interfere with his work. And he expects the same from everyone else." He opened the door for Talbot.

"Come into my office!" Murphy said, frowning like a black thunderhead as soon as Talbot appeared in the pressroom. The managing editor turned to lead the way.

"Hey," the copy boy yelled in a high-itched voice, "are you really the same Matt Talbot who ran off from Beecher Island?"

Matt paused and stared at the wide-eyed boy, who probably wasn't over twelve years old.

163

"Who told you that?"

"A bunch of the men been putting odds on whether you was or not."

Talbot's gaze circled the room, taking in the five men who'd ceased what they were doing and looked at him expectantly.

"Pay 'em no mind," Stein said under his breath, urging Talbot toward the editor's office.

A sudden fire of anger flared up in Talbot. Had his stomach not been queasy and his head still dizzy, he might have let it pass. But, being called a coward by a boy and by men he hardly knew, set a torch blazing in his gut. He'd put a stop to this before it got started.

"Who's saying I'm a coward?" he demanded.

Murphy had stopped at his office door and turned around. "Talbot, get in here!"

"Not until I find out who thinks I'm a coward." In spite of normal good sense, a red film of recklessness flamed up before his eyes. Damn the consequences. He meant to have this out here and now.

The men froze in place for several long seconds, the wall clock ticking loudly in the silence.

"You're a mighty strange-acting fella," a burly pressman said, stepping forward, hooking his thumbs in his leather apron. "I calculated you came to work here shortly after that Injun attack happened. I say you're the very same Matt Talbot. Reckon you could win me a gold eagle by owning up to the fact." He smirked over his shoulder at his fellow workers, as if the $10 gold piece was already in his pocket.

Talbot exploded without warning. His fist shot out with the force of a steam piston. The pressman's jaw cracked as his head snapped sideways. Talbot's knuckles stung against the bristled jaw, and the shock of the blow went clear to his shoulder. The pressman collapsed like a sack of sand.

Three of the others jumped for Talbot, pinning his arms and punching. In the kicking, grappling mêlée, all four staggered against the type case, tipping it over and scattering type across the rough planks.

The three men were swinging wildly, slugging each other as often as Talbot, until the tangle of legs tripped on a box and they all went down. Talbot landed hard on his back, head snapping back against the floor. Everything spun crazily in his vision. Stunned, he could barely feel fists raining down on his head and body. Shouting voices sounded from somewhere far away.

Then Murphy's roar cut through the din,

and a gunshot blasted in the confined space. Talbot, ears ringing and senses starting to come back, realized the room had gone suddenly quiet, and the three men had released him. Still on his back, he blinked through a haze of powder smoke.

Stein was dragging one man away by the collar. The big pressman he'd slugged lay unconscious on the floor.

Talbot blinked several more times and his swimming vision steadied. An acrid smell of burned powder assaulted his nose as he pushed himself to a sitting position.

Murphy, like a hairy, black ogre, stood over him, waving a long-barreled Colt, and glared around the room. "Gawd dammit!" he shouted. "You pied the type. It'll take most of the day to pick it up and sort out this mess."

Still unsteady, Talbot got to his feet, hurting in a half dozen places.

"Collect your pay, Talbot," Murphy roared. "You're fired!"

That was the least of his concerns at the moment as his tender stomach suddenly rebelled and he retched up sour-tasting water onto Murphy's polished boots.

■ ■ ■ ■

PART TWO

■ ■ ■ ■

CHAPTER TEN

Feb. 19, 1870
United States Mint
Carson City, Nevada

At 7:50 P.M. former Sergeant Jacob Mc-Call, swinging a shuttered brass lantern, strode along the deserted corridor, his boots clumping on the stone floor. "Damned mausoleum," he muttered, his steamy breath visible in the yellow lamplight reflecting from the wall sconces.

He paused and fumbled a large ring of keys from his belt to unlock the director's office door. The clerks had gone home hours ago, as had the director, Norman Whitley. Whitley's vacated office retained some warmth from an earlier fire whose red embers still peeked from beneath wood ashes on the hearth.

McCall stepped to the barred window. Nothing was visible but two specks of light from the city. He unsheathed his lantern and held it up to the window. Heavy snow whirled past, some flakes melting on the outside of the glass. His rugged, bent-nose visage stared dimly back at him from the reflection on the thick pane. Gusting wind, driving a blizzard before it off the mountains, howled around a corner of the sandstone building. The dim keening rose and sank, causing him to shiver at the mournful sound. It roused a memory of his grandmother's spinning wheel — a sound he hadn't heard since he was a boy thirty years before. Staring at the image in his mind's eye, he shifted uncomfortably, thinking how quickly time was passing and how little he had to show for it. He'd taken his discharge from the cavalry and tried to cash in on the silver and gold flowing from the Washoe region of Nevada. But he found he'd arrived a bit late to get in on the discoveries and claims that others had already staked, recorded, and dug up, making them millionaires. Hundreds of other men like himself were grubbing for a living at menial jobs. But he considered himself a cut above all those men. It galled him that he was working for poor government wages as captain of the watch, a chief security job at the two-year old United States Branch Mint at Carson City, Nevada.

He set the lantern on the floor to close and latch the inside shutters, then went to the hearth where he fastened the fire screen so no sparks could escape.

His time would come; he was sure of it. Something better awaited him than a wage that barely kept him fed and clothed. Besides, he had no illusions about his job being secure. Many high-placed businessmen, whose money interests lay in San Francisco, had opposed building this branch mint close to the source of gold and silver ore. The first director, Abraham Curry, had resigned six months ago under fire, rumors of embezzlement swirling around him. Now this Norman Whitley was the second political appointee. Workers here could be fired on any whim, and be replaced if the party in power changed with the next national election.

McCall supervised two other security men: Ed Vore and Tom Cowan. They divided the twenty-four-hour day with him. All had the same duties, but McCall, as the supervisor, earned a few dollars more a week. They wore badges and gun belts, but uniforms were not required, thus saving the Treasury Department a little added expense.

He went out, locking the director's office door, and started along the cold corridor leading to the vault.

Ed Vore, a young, fair-haired man, turned the corner and came toward him, coat slung over one shoulder. "Thought I heard you, boss."

"Everything quiet?"

"Yup. She's your baby until four in the morning." Vore slipped into his heavy coat with a hood. "Sure glad you volunteered for the graveyard shift. I don't do well late at night. Guess my body knows that's the time for sleep."

McCall silently accepted credit for his generosity. He'd never mention his working the night shift kept him from Washoe saloons, for which he had a great fondness. Even now he licked his lips, thinking the sweet, warm taste of a whiskey would go down easily this winter night. "Careful going home," he cautioned. "Blowing like hell out there. Easy to get disoriented and lost."

"It's only a mile, and I can use the saloon lights to guide me." Vore waved a gloved hand and disappeared down the hall toward the side door.

McCall waited until he heard the door slam and lock behind Vore. Then he hefted his lantern and moved down the hall toward the vault.

A patent combination lock secured the

steel, counterbalanced vault door. But, as captain of the watch, he had keys and combinations to every door and cabinet and storage bin in the building. He and the director were the only ones not required to log in and out when entering and leaving the vault. He carefully worked the combination; it was so routine, he could have done it in his sleep. His rounds and inspection of every room in the big, two-story building never revealed any surprises. Fire from open flames in the lamps and grates were the biggest danger — although there was little to burn. A robbery was nearly out of the question, especially on a night like this when the god of winter was roaring.

Thunk! Thick bolts slid back when he pulled the big handle. He swung the door open and stepped over the sill. Holding up the lantern he began inspecting the stuffy chamber. Bins of newly minted coins were arranged down the center of the room. They'd been sorted, counted, and tied up in heavy, canvas bags to await dispersal when the schedule called for it, and the weather cleared enough to ship the coinage by train or Wells, Fargo express. It was all too familiar to him and offered little to see. As he went through the same procedure every night, he couldn't keep his mind from wandering. He walked around the room, glancing at everything, smelling the dusty staleness. Not even any air vents in here.

He was starting out the door when his eye caught a lump in a corner of the room. Holding up his lantern, he peered into the dim recesses. Just a wooden sorting table with a tarp thrown over it. Funny how one could see something every day and never take note of it. He paused, trying to recall workmen using that table to sort and count and bag. He could not.

Walking back to the corner, he yanked the tan canvas cover off and dropped it on the floor. It wasn't a table at all, but a wooden crate, the shape of a coffin, but shorter and deeper. It rested on a wooden pallet so the top was nearly waist high. But what caught his eye immediately were the large letters stenciled in black on the side of the crate. They read: *Winchester Repeating Arms Co.* A case of rifles? Here? Three months earlier, during a public ceremony to celebrate Whitley's appointment as director, the Nevada governor had presented him with an engraved 1866 Winchester. Maybe Whitley had additionally been given a whole case of Winchester rifles. Or perhaps he'd bought them on his own, planning to resell them at a profit, and had only stored them here for safe keeping.

The lid of the crate was secured by a brass padlock hanging through a thick hasp. On the face of the big padlock was red sealing wax, imprinted with the director's personal seal. A card tacked atop the crate bore an admonition in block letters: *Sealed by Order of the Superintendent, Jan. 20, 1870. To Be Opened only by Norman Whitley or his appointee.*

He held the lantern close to the padlock. Imprinted in the red sealing wax were the initials *NW,* surrounded by the words: *U.S. Mint Carson City.* It was Whitley's personal seal. Strange. If this was the director's personal property, McCall had no business tampering with it. On the other hand, as captain of the watch, he had responsibility for everything inside the mint. And this was something he knew nothing about — yet. He wanted no mysteries on his watch, he decided. Leaving the vault open, he retreated toward Whitley's office. From a velvet-lined box in a file cabinet he obtained the director's brass seal and stick of red sealing wax. He stuffed the seal and wax into a small pouch, along with the morning newspaper from the director's desk, then returned to the box in the vault.

Spreading the newspaper on the floor

under the lock, he melted the wax with his lantern, letting it drip onto the paper. The standard-issue brass padlock opened easily with his skeleton key.

By the time he'd finished, he was breathing heavily, and was no longer cold. When he started to lift the lid, the hinges creaked loudly in the stillness. He stopped and whirled around, dropping the lid and reaching for his holstered gun. Was someone in the corridor? He held his breath, but heard only his heart thumping in his ears.

"Getting jumpy," he muttered, returning to his task.

He threw back the lid and thrust the lantern inside, expecting to see rows of the brass "yellow boy" receivers of the 1866 Winchesters. Instead, there were only rows and rows of cylindrical sausages, sewn into burlap. Sausages? He picked one up — and it nearly slipped from his fingers from the weight. "Damn!" Setting it on the floor, he pulled out his clasp knife and slit the stitching. Several gold double eagles spilled out, ringing on the stone floor. He swallowed hard, and picked up and pocketed six of them. This would take a little more inspection. Setting the lantern where he could see inside the box, he counted ninety-four sausage-size tubes of about fifty coins each.

A quick mental calculation — 4,700 $20 gold pieces equaled $94,000!

Leaving the vault open, he retreated to the director's office, closed and locked the door, and lit the desk lamp, turning up the wick. He sat in Whitley's chair and opened the middle desk drawer to obtain a square of black velvet and a magnifying glass he'd seen Whitley use many times. Spreading the velvet under the bright light, he laid out the six coins to examine closely. They bore the sheen of new, uncirculated $20 dollar gold pieces. On the reverse, the *CC* mint mark appeared just below the spread eagle. Each feather was sharp and distinct. Around the inside of the rim were the words: *United States of America Twenty D.*

The obverse was a different story. They were all dated 1869, but the classic head of Liberty was pocked with the same small indentations in the same place on each coin, as if there had been an imperfection in the die stamp. In addition, each head and the inside edge of the rim bore a faint shadow of outline as if the die had hit and bounced — the classic mark of a misstrike. One at a time, he held each coin sideways to the light. The milled edge was perfect, but the coin varied ever so slightly in thickness from one side to the other. The gold metal sheets had not been rolled out to the exact thickness required by regulation. That had to be a mistake by the workmen; the rolling presses were less than a year old and could not yet be worn to unevenness. When Whitley took over as director, he'd replaced the workmen in the mint with inexperienced men of his own choosing — men who needed a job in repayment for political loyalty. Nepotism at its worst. But McCall didn't care; this was only a short stop on his way to wealth.

Were these coins listed on the record as being stored? Releasing poor quality gold coins into circulation would damage the reputation of the mint and its new director. Why, then, weren't they immediately melted down and new ones struck? They were dated last year, so they'd existed for several months. What did the official record show? He finally found his key to the file cabinet that held the records of minting and disbursement. He opened the file and, flipping through the sheets, found the one he needed, and ran his finger down the column. *September 17, 1869 $20 gold 4,672 produced 4,666 shipped Distribution complete September 26, 1869.* It was standard procedure to hold back a few samples of each minting.

He sat back in the desk chair, his breath

whistling through his teeth in a long sigh. The official record had been falsified. He recognized the signature of Norman Whitley at the bottom of the sheet. Maybe Whitley didn't know what he was signing. Not likely, since his official seal was impressed into the wax on the lock. McCall tapped his fingers on the desk. He and the director were the only ones who had access to that brass seal.

What now? He had several choices. He could return the coins, reseal the box, and pretend he never saw it — and continue to draw his paltry salary until ousted by the next change of administration. He could take a few coins to supplement his earnings. No, they would surely be missed and he would be the only suspect. Instead of taking a few coins, he'd lift a complete roll. That way, they'd all have to be counted to see if one was missing. He could further deface any coins he spent so they'd appear as if run over by a wagon or scuffed by gravel or rough handling.

Since Whitley had faked the official record, it was obvious he'd squirreled away these coins to enrich himself. With his connections he could easily have them melted down into small ingots. Misstrikes were rare, so their numismatic value could be many times the face value of the coins. Perhaps Whitley intended to release them, a few at a time, onto the collectors' market in the big Eastern cities.

The wind moaned around the corner of the building and down the rock chimney. He shivered, not so much from the cold as from the thought of what his future held — eventual old age and sickness from too much drink. No family, no money. Begging in the street until he was found frozen some night. It was a bleak picture that would likely never come to reality, but his imagination always seemed to conjure up the worst possibilities. This could be the angel of opportunity smiling on him. And if he didn't grasp her hand quickly, she'd be gone, never to return. This was found money, unaccounted for, that he could scoop up and run with. It's not like anyone would be hurt by it. The miners and owners had been paid for the ore; the mill workers had been paid for crushing and smelting it into bars; men at the mint had been paid for rolling and minting it into coins. The director had recorded it as being disbursed to banks and into circulation. Yet, there it was — collecting dust in the vault, apparently unwanted by anyone, as if it'd been dumped back into the ground from whence it came. From childhood onward, logic had always been his ally when it came to taking something that didn't belong to him.

He carefully returned everything to the desk drawer and file cabinet, locked them, put out the lamp, and returned it to its place. Then he exited the office with the newspaper, the brass seal, and a stick of red sealing wax. Time to take a pocketful of these marred beauties for expenses. One tube of fifty coins would do it — an even $1,000. Then he'd seal the box with its remaining ninety-three tubes of coins at fifty double eagles per tube and begin the second phase of his plan. Whistling "Camptown Races" softly to himself, he was amazed at how quickly his prospects had brightened.

CHAPTER ELEVEN

May 8, 1870
Gold Hill, Nevada

Matthew Talbot's eyes flew open when he sensed the change in vibrations through the floor of the freight car. The train was slowing to a stop. If they were pulling off on a siding to let another train pass, he'd stay aboard. But if they were approaching a water tank or a depot, he'd have to get off — fast. The brakeman, swinging the short club he used as a leverage tool for turning the brake wheels, would be checking the cars along the short train; a free rider was sure to be discovered. Recent bruises had educated him about railroad men's stance toward tramps. Brakemen took a proprietary attitude toward their trains, even when a poor itinerant was making no trouble and occupying only a small space in an empty freight or ore car.

He fingered the loaded .32 Smith & Wesson revolver, snug in its holster in his jacket pocket. It was for last-resort self-defense. He wanted no confrontation with this Virginia & Truckee train crew.

He threw off his threadbare blanket and crept to the partially open side door. A cold draft was blowing in. Carefully poking his head out, he looked forward. A curve in the track allowed him to see the locomotive approaching a high trestle. So they weren't stopping, after all. Down the hill below, frame buildings were scattered along both sides of a gulch and up the hills. That would be Gold Hill, and the upcoming trestle was likely the Crown Point Trestle, bridging a major gulf between Gold Hill and the larger town of Virginia City he could see two miles ahead.

He'd never been to either place, but they fit the description given to him the night before by another knight of the road in a desert camp. He, his informant, and two other men had been sharing a roasted prairie chicken spitted over their campfire. Talbot had managed to bring down the wild bird with one shot just as it was nesting for the night in a clump of sage. A mostly lucky shot it was, but he never let on to his fellow tramps. They'd given him due respect for both the food and his skill with a firearm.

He'd supplied the meat, and the others the drink in the form of a bottle, whose contents were too fiery to match what was printed on the label. They'd also furnished him with accurate information about train schedules and geography.

A good place to get off — while the train was moving barely faster than he could walk. He rolled his blanket and slung it over a shoulder, belting it around his body. His only baggage was a scuffed cylindrical leather grip barely two feet long, but large enough to hold a tightly rolled spare shirt, pair of pants, razor, several cotton bandannas, and odds and ends — toothbrush, small scissors, a block of stick matches, a box of .32 cartridges, and the latest of his journal notebooks.

Clasping the grip, he sprang out and away from the car, a safe distance from the deadly wheels. Even though he jumped in the direction of the train's slow movement, and flexed his knees when he hit, he wasn't able to keep his balance and stumbled and rolled down the slight embankment, sliding to a stop in two inches of wet snow. *A soft but sloppy landing,* he thought, climbing back up the bank, brushing the snow and mud from his pants and butt. He looked after the caboose and empty ore cars of the departing train that rattled on across the trestle toward Virginia City.

Life could be good, he thought, inhaling a deep breath of fresh air as he turned south along the rails, stepping on the ties. A warm breeze from the southeast shredded the plumes from several dozen smokestacks, carrying the choking air away from him. The gold and silver that miners tore from the earth was being extracted at a price. From his vantage point on the ridge, he scanned the peaceful-looking town below, and wondered idly how many men there died of lung ailments, of whiskey, of gun and knife wounds, of syphilis, of mountain fever, or mine accidents. From what he'd heard of the towns along the Comstock Lode, the mortality rate was higher than any other place of similar size.

He let the thought slide away in the peace of the morning while sunshine warmed his face. Rivulets of water streamed in all directions as two inches of snow rapidly melted. The fierce god of winter was grudgingly retreating into the mountains, finally allowing spring to creep up from the south and lay her gentle hand on this barren landscape. Perhaps he'd started north too early from his small cabin on eastern edge of Death Valley.

Following the fiasco in Denver sixteen months ago, he'd worked as a tramp printer in a dozen small towns, honing his skills as a compositor, learning more of the trade. During the dark, cold days of December, just before Christmas, he'd taken the train to St. Louis to visit his mother. He'd found her somewhat thinner and grayer than the last time he'd been home, but she was well and happy, working as a maid in the homes of several wealthy families, and tutoring the ten-year-old daughter of the president of a textile company. On her own time, she socialized with several good friends at church. She assured him she lacked for nothing.

Was she just putting up a brave front for him? No. She'd always been honest with him. "I brought you a little Christmas gift," he said, opening the small grip he'd set on the floor next to his chair. "I wore these when I escaped from Beecher Island," he said, handing her a pair of doeskin moccasins.

"Oh, they're lovely," she said, caressing the soft hide and running her fingers over the red-and-green porcupine quill pattern.

"I've been told they're from the Northern Cheyenne tribe." He was glad she didn't ask how he'd acquired them. "I walked a long way in them, and had to have a cobbler reinforce the soles with leather and stitch up the seams, too."

"I'll wear them for slippers to keep my feet warm in this drafty old house." She unlaced her shoes and slipped the moccasins on her feet. "*Ah,* like walking on the clouds, they're that soft," she said, getting up and taking a few steps. "I'll think of you every time I wear them."

Talbot smiled at her obvious pleasure and the lilting dialect she still retained after all these years in America.

"I'm working toward teaching myself the printer's trade, taking jobs here and there on newspapers."

"That's good. A man needs a skill so he'll always have work. There were too many common laborers in Ireland."

"That's all past now," he said. "A long time ago for us."

"You were born there," she reminded him, "though it's little you remember about it, I'm sure. It was my home, too, growing up. Good memories of traipsin' the wind-swept hills of Kerry, pickin' wildflowers, outings with m' classmates." Her face relaxed into a dreamy expression. "And later, when I met your father. *Ah . . .* not another like him, I'm thinkin', he was that handsome and strong. There was hard work aplenty for both of us after we married, but happy times, too, lookin' back." She sighed. "Then the Great Hunger took him, and most of our kin, too, save a few that were able to emigrate. Now scattered who knows where. Well, the Lord takes, as well as gives, as I'm sure you've learned by now." She stared somberly at an icon of the Virgin and Child on the wall, apparently conjuring up visions of earlier times. Then she brightened. "But the Lord smiled on the pair of us, now, didn't He? Brought us safe to this blessed land. We must always be thankful for that." She got up to set their empty teacups on the drain board. "You're all I have left in this world, now," she said. "Maybe, when you become a master printer, you can get a job here in Saint Louis. But no matter where you are or what you're doing, I want to hear from you."

He swallowed hard, hardly knowing how to respond. It had been months since he'd heard such kind words.

"Remember that you and I come from hardy Irish stock. We must do whatever it takes to survive. Do good to everyone, and make me proud. But don't allow evil men or politicians to push you into jeopardizing your life needlessly for political reasons or for money. You survived that terrible war, and that Indian attack. From now on, make good choices and take care of yourself."

He nodded, thinking his decision to leave Beecher Island had been a good one.

"I baked soda bread this morning," she said brightly, changing the subject as if she sensed his embarrassment at her loving words. "How'd you like some corned beef and cabbage for supper to go with it?"

"I'd love it."

Three days later he took the train west, much more relaxed and easier in his mind. It was a trip he was glad he'd made.

He replayed this scene in his mind as he walked along the tracks, feeling an inner glow that warmed him against the external chill.

Thoughts of the Beecher Island battle had gradually receded, even though he still had an occasional nightmare about it. In the bad dreams, he usually saw himself back on that accursed island, lying in a rifle pit. Whooping, painted warriors were attacking on horseback. Bullets stung his arms and legs. He fired at them with his Spencer, but it jammed. He looked around for help, but none of the other scouts was there; he was all alone. Black-bearded Murphy, his Denver editor, rose from one of the trenches with a blood-curdling laugh that cut through the roar of gunfire and the piercing screams. Sometimes he could see Phil Granger in a nearby trench, wounded, but was unable to reach him. His own arms and legs seemed to weigh a hundred pounds each; he couldn't move to assist his friend. He usually awoke with a start, perspiring. It took a minute or so for his pounding heart to slow as he realized the terrible scene was only clutter from the storehouse of his memory.

He sat down on one of the rails, took up a nearby stick, and scraped the mud off his boots, then rubbed handfuls of snow to clean them still further. His wet pants legs would dry in the warm breeze. The dirt of traveling was just one of the hazards of being an itinerant printer. Most editors referred to men like him as tramp printers — skilled workmen who were apparently increasing in number throughout the West.

Talbot brushed his hands on his pants and stared into space. He'd run into several tramp printers during the past three summers — vagabonds, like himself, who wanted no ties. Many of them were just out to see the world, some nursing an addiction to alcohol, unable to hold a steady job for whatever reason, or fleeing a wife back East. He'd found their company stimulating, since a few spoke more than one language, were very literate, and took their jobs as play. His one regret as he traveled around was the scarcity of books. When he could beg, borrow, or buy them, they were heavy to carry, but he valued their weight more than gold.

He stood and hefted his grip again. A place the size of Gold Hill was bound to support at least one daily paper. He'd find it and apply for work. If there was no opening, he'd hike on over to Virginia City. A town of 25,000 probably had a dozen papers. The residents of these remote towns hungered for more than just local news, he'd discovered. With recent access to both telegraph and railroad, the newspapers here could dish up recent national news everyday as well. In a population continually in flux, he was confident he'd quickly find a job.

Until now, he'd delayed coming to the Comstock because of its reputation as an especially bloody place where life had little value. It was also notorious for it's unpredictable weather. Sudden, severe extremes of heat, sleet, hail, screaming windstorms and blizzards were common here, unlike more temperate climates where a layer of humidity cushioned the harshness of the changes. He'd visited and worked in such locations — small towns on the eastern edge of the plains, meeting all kinds of people, plying his trade, perfecting his skills. Now it was time to tackle the wild towns of the Comstock. He started down the slope into the cauldron of Gold Hill.

CHAPTER TWELVE

May 30, 1870
Yellow Jacket Mine
Gold Hill, Nevada
Brrrooommm!

The three miners paused as one and lowered their picks and shovels as the drawn-out roar reverberated down the long empty tunnels.

"What was that?" Phil Granger breathed, staring at his two fellow miners. The glow from the coal-oil lantern cast their grimy, wide-eyed faces in soft, yellow light.

"That warn't no blast," Robbie Welsh averred.

"More like a cave-in," bandy-legged Billingsgate remarked, leaning his pick against the wall and pulling out a filthy bandanna to wipe his face.

Granger, glad for a break from shoveling broken rock from the face of the drift, put his hand on the rim of the ore car, and cocked his head to catch any more sound, but heard only a lingering soft rattle of falling débris or loose rock. "Sounds like ore sliding down a metal chute," he finally said.

"Came from somewhere up above," Welsh said.

"Ain't nobody working up there," Billingsgate said. "Those tunnels near the surface been worked out and abandoned for a good while."

They stared silently at each other, speculating.

"Reckon the engineers knew these mountains were gonna settle down sooner or later and fill up the empty spaces we dug out," Billingsgate added.

"I'd just as soon they didn't, as long as I'm down here," Granger said, taking a deep breath of the dust-laden air, as if oxygen were in short supply.

"That didn't sound like any cave-in I ever heard," Welsh said.

"Reckon we better get outta here, just in case," Billingsgate said. "Head for the lift. Our shift's nearly up anyhow."

That was all Granger wanted to hear. He snatched up the lantern and was three strides down the tunnel before the man finished speaking.

The other two were right on his heels. The

main shaft was at least a half mile from where they'd been working and required two turns. Just before they made the second left turn, the strong draft of air down the passageway brought a slight smell of smoke. Granger's stomach contracted at this danger signal. He said nothing, but started to run, stumbling against the ore car rails, turning his ankle on loose rock. They were still at least four hundred yards from the lift. Light from the swinging oil lantern shivered the blackness into flashes and flickers of light, bouncing off the shiny, wet walls between thick, splintering support timbers. He blocked out the realization that thousands of tons of rock were pressing down on the fragile timbering.

The odor didn't seem to be from burning wood or gas. It smelled more like smoldering trash and garbage. He sprinted faster, panting, his throat burning and raw from the thickening tendrils of gray-white smoke twisting in the light of the jiggling lantern.

It was the longest quarter mile he'd ever run. His lungs cried for air and he thought he couldn't go another ten steps. He finally dropped to his hands and knees below the worst of the smoke and crawled as fast as he could move, tearing his pants and bruising his knees.

Suddenly the three men stumbled from the mouth of the tunnel into the main shaft where the air was somewhat cleaner. Granger rolled upright, gasping. They were still a thousand feet below the surface, but at least the cage hoist was here, resting on the platform just above the sump. He yanked the signal cord. He couldn't hear the bell, but prayed the hoist operator wasn't asleep or drunk.

The three miners slid open the cage door and rushed in. The door clanged shut and the cage jerked into motion, sliding upward on its greased tracks.

None of the men spoke as the cage continued to ascend — fifty feet, a hundred, two hundred. Rocky walls slid past next to the latticework of the cage. The air grew noticeably cooler and cleaner. Granger drew a deep lungful of fresh air, removed his helmet, and wiped a sleeve across his sweaty forehead. They'd just been snatched from the bowels of hell, and he knew it. The signal bell sounded from above as other miners reached the bottom of the main shaft and rang for the cage lift.

As the cage neared the surface, daylight streamed down on them, and he heard another bell in the distance — the frantic clanging of the fire alarm from a third story tower above Engine Company No. 2.

"Nine men are missing," Granger said. "They were working on the third level."

"One of them is Peter Hager," Billingsgate said, his normally bright face grim in the light of the overhead Rochester lamp. McKinnon's Saloon was blocked from afternoon sunlight by stores that abutted both sides of the building.

"Damned lucky we were to get to the hoist," Granger said, a chill traveling up his back at the thought they might never have seen the light of day again. Instead, three hours later, here they were, washed clean of sweat and smoke and dust, leaning on the end of a bar near the free lunch. Granger picked at a piece of boiled egg, while Billingsgate was into his second beer, ignoring the food entirely.

The short, bandy-legged miner sipped the foam. "One of the worst I ever seen. And I seen some bad ones."

Silence fell like a sack of lead weights between each utterance.

"Warn't no fault o' the mine owners," the little man added.

"In a way it was," Granger said. "The tunnels were run within fifteen feet of the surface, just under the dry goods store."

"That was years ago, likely before that store was even built." Billingsgate took a long swallow of his beer. "What I can't figure is why the whole thing caught fire today."

"I heard a fireman say the store had a supply of matches and a few barrels of black powder on hand. When the store collapsed into the mine, she just ignited. Nothing but the façade left standing, and they'll have to tear that down before it falls." Granger finished his beer and held up his glass for a refill. "Damn' near everything in life is a matter of distance and time. The owners knew the building was shifting and cracking, and were planning to move all the merchandise out today."

"They were a day late."

"And it cost several lives plus a helluva lot of money."

"Hear tell they didn't have a dime's worth of insurance."

"How long you reckon they'll have to blast steam into the tunnels?" Granger asked, laying down a ten-cent piece for his beer.

"Billingsgate pursed his lips. "Two . . . three days, at least, if a lot of that dry timbering is on fire, too."

"Then they've given up getting anyone else out alive."

Billingsgate nodded. He turned away, but not before Granger saw tears welling up in his eyes.

At that moment, Granger resolved never to go underground to work again. He'd draw his pay and look for another job. He distracted himself by eyeing a whore across the room whose back was to them. Anything to keep from thinking about the disaster — the kind of horrible accident that was all too frequent in Washoe mines.

"I'm through mining," Granger said.

"How long you been at it? Four months? Six months?"

"Going on a year. I worked at the Crown Point before this," Granger said.

"*Humph!* I been at it twelve years come next month. Wonder how many tons of ore I've moved in my life?" He flexed a bicep and grinned.

"In just my short ten months, I've actually seen or heard about damned near everything . . . men falling down mine shafts and busting their brains out, men falling into sump water and dragged out weeks later with no flesh left, men crushed by cave-ins, blown to bits by premature explosions, dead from heat exhaustion, flayed by live steam, crushed between cages and the shaft wall." He drew a deep breath. "How many miners ever live long enough to die in bed?"

"I reckon the few who do have their lungs full of rock dust," Billingsgate said, the grin fading. If the hazards of his profession worried him, he kept it to himself. "A man gets to worrying about little things, or stuff that might never happen, he soon gets scared of his own shadow, wondering when his time's coming." He gestured toward the bartender. "Hell, even tendin' bar ain't safe. Liable to catch a stray bullet 'most any night. Or some drunk takes a dislike to you for short-changing him. You could catch some kinda rot from one o' them whores. Even writing up the news can get you killed if somebody doesn't like what you say about them." He gulped a long swallow of beer as if to wash down the world's hazards. He burped. "If a man's scared o' living, he oughtn't get outta bed in the morning . . . especially if he lives in Gold Hill or Virginia City. This ain't no place for the faint o' heart."

"I'm working hard to develop your attitude," Granger said dryly. He chose not to think the little man was taking a stab at him for quitting.

"Where else but in the mines is a man gonna earn four dollars a shift — thanks to the Miners' Union?" Billingsgate continued.

200

"Nowhere I know of, if a man sits below the salt."

"Huh?"

"Nothing. Just an old expression meaning if you're not one of the wealthy, $4 for eight hours is about the best a fella can do."

"You're darn' right it's good pay. Dangerous work, though," he admitted, "but I already got me a nest egg saved up for my old age."

"Not wishing you any bad luck, but put me in your will," Granger said. He was already thinking ahead, wondering if he should try for another laboring job.

As if reading his thoughts, Billingsgate asked: "What'd you do afore you took up mining?"

"Worked for the Kansas-Pacific Railroad. Grading crew," Granger replied.

"Why'd you quit?"

"Didn't. Got laid off when the Injuns attacked the work gangs. They didn't cotton to us putting a railroad across what they considered their land."

"So the rail line never got finished."

"Oh, yeah, it was finished later, I just never went back." He stopped short of explaining why — the scouting party under Colonel George Forsyth, the attacks by the massed tribes of warriors, the siege on

Beecher Island in the middle of the Arikaree River, the piles of stinking dead horses,
the starving, the fear. Even though twenty
months in the past, the experience flooded
his memory with vivid, painful detail, and
he could not talk objectively about it. He
understood now why many veterans of the
late war were reticent about their soldier-
ing.

Billingsgate was looking at him expectantly, the whites around his blue eyes
veined with red from dust and smoke.

"After I rode with Forsyth's Scouts, I just
went on to other things."

The miner's eyes widened. "You was one
of Forsyth's Scouts?"

"Yeah." Granger had hoped the little man
wasn't aware of them. He should have
stopped short of mentioning Forsyth's
name.

Billingsgate looked at him with new respect. "Ain't no wonder you want to quit
mining. You done used up two or three of
your nine lives already. I heard that business was pretty bad."

"The papers made it out to be a lot more
dramatic than it was," Granger said with a
dismissive shrug. "We just took it minute by
minute, hour by hour, day by day, and did
what had to be done to stay alive. Like you

do in the mine."

Billingsgate nodded at the apt simile.

Granger drank two more beers to justify filling up on the free lunch of bread, cheese, and eggs. In late afternoon he left as the saloon was beginning to get crowded. He'd see the Yellow Jacket foreman in the morning and draw his time. What money he'd managed to save would tide him over for about two weeks until he could find work elsewhere.

Trudging to his boarding house, he thought of his mining stock, a hundred twenty shares he'd bought weeks ago at $27 per share. He'd sell that, but dare he sell it now? The last he looked, it was down to $18. But if he hung onto it, it could drop still further. Speculation in mining stock was a sport on the Washoe; everyone indulged in it, from swampers in saloons to whores, preachers, and newspaper editors. Some made profits, some lost. It was a chancy business, a form of gambling mania that had seized the entire population. He himself didn't have gambler's instincts, the willingness to lose as well as win. Money came too hard to risk it on the turn of a card or the luck of finding rich ore. Or was it luck? Men who were wealthy and powerful, like Sharon, one of the owners of the

Virginia & Truckee Railroad and of the Consolidated Virginia, had not become rich by chance. Being knowledgeable traders who had inside information about mines and veins of ore, they conspired to manipulate stock.

For all the rest of the poor working people, buying stock was like buying a ticket on the Brooklyn lottery, that was operating even this far West. At the moment, he had two tickets for this lottery in his pocket, and the monthly drawing was tonight. He'd tried everything to make money in the months he'd been on the Comstock, but with little success. Salaries were generally high, but so were expenses. Everyone here seemed to live as if there were no tomorrow. And, for many, there wasn't. The Virginia City graveyard on the edge of town was filling up fast — with victims of accidents, murders, suicides. He had no intention of becoming one of those forgotten ones who occupied a grave in the dry, rocky soil. If there was one thing he'd learned from his old friend, Matt Talbot, life held more than just work, sleep, food, and more work, interspersed with little pleasure. There was literature, and the theater, and music, and great books to read, philosophy to discuss, loyal friendships to develop.

He clumped up the outside steps to his second-floor room, wondering what'd happened to Talbot. It was still a mystery to him why his friend had left that night. If he'd only waited two more nights, the two of them could have gone together — after Forsyth gave them all the chance to escape. Yet . . . none of the others had opted to go, even then. They'd all shouted down the very notion. It was foolish bravado, in Granger's opinion, although some of the able-bodied had to stay and look after the wounded. Strange how things worked out. By leaving two days early, Talbot had done something the newspapers called "dishonorable." This was due mostly to what Sergeant Jacob McCall had told reporters. Jake McCall — the very name of the man set his teeth on edge.

CHAPTER THIRTEEN

"Talbot!" Alfred Doten, owner and chief editor of *The Gold Hill Morning News*, crooked a finger at him from the outside doorway.

"What'd I do now?" Talbot muttered to himself, setting aside his composing stick and wiping his hands on a rag. He glanced at the foreman, who was giving him a look of curiosity.

Talbot stepped toward the door in response to Doten's summons, thinking the foreman would probably be down on him the rest of the day for making up to the boss. It was always one damned thing or another. He'd been here four weeks — longer than his usual stint — and was thinking of moving on. Office politics and jealousies were one of the hazards of a regular job.

"Sir?"

The two men stepped outside into the

sunshine, and Doten shut the door on the rhythmic hissing and clanking of the small, steam-powered press.

"I have to take the omnibus over to Virginia City to run *The Territorial Enterprise* for now. Dan DeQuille, the editor, has been dismissed again for being drunk." He sighed. "Anyway, I need your help to cover the story of that mass prison break down in Carson City early this morning."

Talbot thrilled at the prospect, but only said: "Be glad to, but I thought you had a local down there."

"I inherited that reporter two months ago when I bought the paper from Lynch's widow. But the Carson local writes like he's only half literate. And he never seems to get all the facts for a good news story."

Talbot nodded, knowing he was being given the chance to show what he could do beyond just typesetting. "I'll leave right now," he said.

"This is a big story, so give it your best. Fifty-four men broke out of the state prison. Killed six guards who tried to stop them. Wounded several more, including the lieutenant governor, who happened to be there conferring with the warden."

"Damn. Any of them been caught?"

"That's what you need to find out. The

Vigilance Committee has come to the fore in Virginia City to help the police. They've pretty much taken over the town to protect the citizens. No one messes with the vigilantes around there."

Talbot jerked his head toward the pressroom. "You clear this with the foreman?"

"Don't worry about him. I'm the boss here." Alf Doten's expression softened; his grin split the gap between mustache and goatee, showing strong white teeth. "I've seen a few of the items you've written. And I plan to find a slot for one or two of your shorter poems. You have a natural feel for words, and I'm hoping I can talk you into staying on here."

Talbot could feel himself flushing, and it wasn't just the heat of the June sun on his face. "Thank you."

"I know talent when I see it."

"As to staying on. . . ."

"We'll talk about that later. You need some money?" He dug into his vest pocket. "Here's an advance on next week's salary." He thrust a double eagle into Talbot's hand. "Take the noon cars down to Carson, get the story, and be back here by suppertime. I'll still be at the *Enterprise,* but write up the story and leave it on my desk. Don't worry about length." He paused. "Better

208

yet, set it in type and I'll read the proof. That'll save time. Since the morning paper has already gone to press, I'll get out an extra tomorrow with this as the lead story." He turned away, then swung around. "No promise, mind you, but if you do a good job with this, you could be my regular local reporter and I'll fill in behind you with another compositor. Your salary will go up from thirty dollars to thirty-six a week."

Talbot couldn't suppress a grin. This forty-one-year-old publisher didn't hesitate to make quick decisions and act on them. How could he not like a man who enjoyed all the pleasures of life, including work? He went to the theater at least five times a week, escorting his mistress, a grass widow he'd taken up with. According to rumors in the pressroom, this Mrs. M., as she was referred to, was as plain-looking as a sack of turnips, but made up for it by being always available and willing. Doten himself was held in awe as a man with the durability of a machine that never wound down. He was a member of a volunteer fire company, often called to duty at all hours of the day or night, was active in politics, cruised the saloons with actors, actresses, and ladies of the evening, drinking until the early hours of the morning. He attended all the socials held by every church, lodge hall, union, and patriotic club, went to funerals and weddings, witnessed post mortems, examined mines, and speculated in stock. And he still found time to operate two newspapers, writing articles and poetry, and keep an eye on a dozen or so employees. Hours for sleep were short and irregular. Talbot wondered how long the man could last at such a pace.

Looking out the window of the slow-moving train, Talbot pondered this different mode of travel compared to the way he'd entered town a few weeks earlier on a Virginia & Truckee boxcar. The Battle of Beecher Island, as it'd become known, had been a turning point in his life. Since then, he wasn't inclined to provide for the morrow. He'd never been much for planning ahead, anyway. Before that terrible encounter, he'd drifted from job to job, only vaguely proposing to become a journeyman printer someday. But since Beecher Island, he'd completely lapsed into living in the moment. He was only twenty-seven years old, but had seen ample evidence that life was short so why waste it worrying about the future? He usually let things happen, then reacted to them. Perhaps he'd get into something more permanent by the time he was thirty. As long as he kept going in the one general direction of printing and publishing, the future would take care of itself, and he'd wind up as a master printer or editor. For now, he'd focus on the immediate task before him. And that task was getting the story of the prison break at Carson City. The other passengers in the car were abuzz with the news, and, from the conversations he could hear, most of them were on their way to Carson to view the site of the violence and carnage like people were drawn to a train wreck. Doten's extra tomorrow would be sold out, no matter how many copies he chose to print.

The train made slow, cautious progress, negotiating the twisting inclines between Gold Hill and Carson. But, as a man who savored the moment, Talbot didn't care how long the trip took. Comfortable in the plush seat, he enjoyed the ride and looked around at the details of the ornate coach, from the brass oil lamps overhead to the intricate geometric patterns painted on the oilcloth-covered ceiling. The windows along the cupola atop the center of the coach were tilted open to admit fresh summer air. He breathed deeply and wished this moment could last forever.

But it didn't. The train chuffed into the

Carson depot at precisely 2:00 in the afternoon.

He grabbed his jacket containing the leather-covered journal he kept with him at all times. He used it not only to record the day's events and to comment on things, but also to jot down snatches of verse as they came to him, and to record creative inspirations and ideas for stories. Every available hack and jitney was quickly snapped up by the debarking passengers. Talbot swung aboard an overloaded horse-drawn hack and hung on by one hand and one foot as it wheeled out and joined the rush of vehicles toward the state prison just outside of town. At least one or two other reporters were likely in the crowd, but Talbot didn't care. He was here to get a story, and would put up his resourcefulness and writing craft against any other newspaperman.

In less than a quarter hour, the sandstone façade of the massive prison loomed up ahead. Several people milled around the main entrance, apparently being kept out by prison officials or the police.

Talbot dropped off the hackney and strode toward the big double doors under the archway, wondering how he'd get inside. Two guards in blue uniforms stood at the door with rifles at parade rest.

He was several hours late, so all the dead and wounded had probably been taken away, even though one extra ambulance remained parked under the trees, its team unhitched and grazing nearby.

Walking boldly up to the guards at the door, he said: "I'm from *The Gold Hill Morning News* and I'd like an interview with the warden."

"You and everybody else," a guard retorted.

"The warden is in the process of writing a formal statement," the other guard said.

Talbot was aware the warden, a political appointee, was subject to being fired if found negligent or somehow at fault in this massive escape. It was no wonder he was being reticent; Talbot knew what it was like to be roasted in the hot light of bad publicity.

He'd make one more stab at this. "Is it true the lieutenant governor was injured in the breakout?" The guards remained silent, staring straight ahead.

Talbot walked away, wondering if such a large escape had torn down a door or gate or even part of the wall. Something had been breached, that was sure. He was certain that any gaps in this stone monolith would be guarded now. About all he could hope for was some second-hand information. But he needed details — at best, an eyewitness account he could dramatize for maximum human interest.

He joined a group of gawkers clustered near a bullet-pocked section of the outer wall streaked with rust-colored blood. One or more had surely been cut down here. He strolled around the corner of the several-acre enclosure, glancing up at the thirty-foot high wall of sandstone blocks. The wall was surmounted at the corners and in the middle by guard towers with Gatling guns. Impressive as it was, it hadn't been able to contain fifty-odd determined criminals.

An iron gate swung outward from a recess in the wall ahead, and a blue-uniformed guard emerged. The gate shut behind him with an authoritative click. The guard strode toward him, head down, the stiff bill of the pillbox cap hiding his face.

Talbot stopped. Maybe he could wring some information out of this man. The guard stalked past him, scowling, not looking up. Talbot got a good view of his profile, the sandy, blond hair curling out from under the cap. He felt a jolt of recognition. "Phil!" he burst out. "Phil Granger!"

The guard jerked to a stop and swung around. His frown slowly faded into a look of wonder. His mouth fell open. "Matt Talbot?"

"The same."

"I wouldn't have thought of you for fifty dollars."

"Too bad. You'd be fifty dollars richer," Talbot said, grinning.

"Lord knows, I could use the money." Granger thrust out his hand with no hesitation and they gripped a firm handshake. "How . . . what . . . ?"

"You a guard here?"

"Was until five minutes ago."

"Quit?"

"Fired."

They stood regarding one another.

"Want to tell me about it?" Talbot asked.

"If you got time."

"Nothing but."

"I'm heading to town to catch the train back to Virginia City."

"I'm with you."

They fell into step together.

"We got a lot of catching up to do." Granger gave him a searching, sideways look as if to reassure himself Talbot wasn't some illusion who'd vanish if ignored for a few seconds.

As they came into view of the crowd milling around the front of the prison, several men rushed up to Granger, all shouting questions. "What can you tell us of the escape?"

"Have any been recaptured?"

"Did they have inside help?"

"Who was the ringleader?"

Granger roughly shoved them aside. "I don't know anything!"

The persistent crowd didn't believe him as they continued to press in. "You're a guard here. Tell us what you know."

"Get out of my way!"

In the pushing and shoving, Talbot was separated, but rushed back in to help claw the eager men away from Granger.

The pair of them finally broke free and the crowd fell back, apparently giving up.

No hacks were available, so Granger, hatless and his tie hanging, walked quickly away in the direction of Carson City. "It's only two miles. We can walk it."

Talbot caught up with him, as Granger pulled off his tie and dropped it. "It'll be that way on the train, too, unless I can ditch this uniform."

"Well, you lost your cap. That's a start."

"Good idea." He shrugged out of the dark blue jacket. "Didn't realize how hot this thing was." His white shirt was damp with sweat.

They walked mostly in silence until they reached the depot, and bought two tickets to Virginia City on the 3:15 that was panting at the platform, ready to depart.

"Mister, can you spare something for an old soldier?" A haggard man with a week's worth of stubble on his sagging cheeks approached them on the platform.

Granger glanced at him. "Which side were you on?"

The tramp straightened perceptibly, a light emanating from watery eyes. "I served in the Army of the Cumberland, suh!"

"Here!" Granger tossed him the uniform jacket. "Wear Union blue in good health."

A blast on the steam whistle drowned any response, and the two men swung aboard the steps of the last coach as the train began to roll.

"You first," Talbot said when they settled in a velvet covered bench seat.

"Had a big row with my supervisor. Wanted to lay blame on me and three other guards for that escape. Hell, I only been there a week. The big bosses have to show they were doing something about the breakout, so they sacrificed a few of us late arrivals. Tried to make it look like our lack of security was the reason." He snorted his contempt. "It was obvious to everyone the escape had been well planned for months." He threw up his hands. "I never wanted to be a prison guard, anyway. It happened to be the first job I could find after I left the mines. Applied at the mint, but there were no openings, even for guards."

"I'm working for *The Gold Hill Morning News.*"

"Oh, yeah . . . Alf Doten. A good man."

"He sent me down here to get the story of this breakout. I'd appreciate any details you can give me. I'll keep your name out of the story if you want."

Granger nodded and proceeded to tell him everything he knew about the largest escape in the prison's history. It wasn't much. The prisoners had erupted before daybreak as they were being marched to breakfast. "The surprise was complete. On a signal, they all attacked the guards at once. We didn't stand a chance. They clubbed us, grabbed our guns, and shot down everyone in their way. I crawled under a table when the shooting started. The Gatling guns in the towers opened up when the prisoners busted out into the yard. But it was so dark, the men on the walls were afraid of hitting the guards the cons were using for hostages."

"Lucky you weren't hit."

"Well, I quit my last job because the prospects for long life weren't good. I'm not afraid of dying, mind you. I just don't want to cash in any sooner than necessary."

"Those prisoners were desperate."

"Mostly lifers in for murder, armed robbery, and such. Hardcases who had nothing to lose." He looked out the coach window. "Now, more than fifty of them are running loose out there somewhere."

For the first time Talbot thought of the menace these escapees might pose to the population, and understood why the Vigilance Committee was an active force in Virginia City. His only concern had been getting the news story. He jotted one more sentence to make sure he had all Granger could tell him and said: "I doubt they're hanging around here, if posses are on their trail. If I were one of them, I'd be for putting distance between myself and that prison."

"Some of them could be hiding on this train," Granger said.

"Maybe, but no threat to us. Murder is generally done in the heat of passion, or because of a grudge. Not many people are killed by total strangers, unless somebody is resisting a robbery, or trying to stop a burglar."

"Or fighting Indians."

The Beecher Island scene flashed into Talbot's memory.

"Nothing personal," Granger said, glancing sideways at him. "Anyway, we'll save all the catching up for tonight. How's about we take in a play? You free to go see *Hamlet* at Swanson's Theater? Show starts at eight, then we'll have dinner and a few drinks. Make a night of it."

"Sure. I'll write up this article and set it in type, and meet you at the theater in Virginia City about half past seven." His rough-edged, blond friend was the least judgmental of men. Slipping back into a friendship was as comfortable as slipping on a pair of well-worn boots.

"Damn, it's good to see your face again!" Granger burst out. "Been wondering for the longest what become o' you."

The two men had barely settled into their plush seats for the third act when the theater was jolted by a concussion and the glass chandeliers swayed dangerously overhead. Before anyone could react, a rolling motion heaved the floor and its rows of seats up and down like a ship in a seaway. The performance stopped and screams erupted in the hall, drowning the rush of feet and the grinding of beams and rafters.

Talbot and Granger jumped from their seats and sprang back against the wall to avoid being trampled by the flood of patrons surging toward the doors.

After a long thirty seconds, the motion stopped, and the two men stumbled out the front door into C Street in the midst of well-dressed theater-goers scattering away from the buildings. Dust rose from the joints of several nearby wooden structures.

"That was no mine blast," Granger panted.

"I've never been in an earthquake before, but nobody had to tell me what that was," Talbot added, looking behind him to make sure he wasn't close to any other buildings. His racing heart was beginning to slow. "Good thing I know how that play ends." He forced a smile.

"Let's go have supper. All that excitement made me hungry."

An hour later, they were stuffing themselves with baked prairie chicken and sweet potatoes, washed down with claret.

They were only half finished with dessert when the restaurant was jolted by two sharp aftershocks. Startled, Talbot dropped his fork, but held his seat during the crashing of glassware as several panicked patrons fled outside. "Good excuse to run out without paying," Granger remarked, calmly wiping his mouth.

"Thought you'd be eating a big, rare steak," Talbot said, to distract himself from his own rising fear of the sudden jolts.

"Haven't eaten red meat since we dined on rare and rotten horse for several days," Granger replied, fingering two silver dollars from his vest pocket. "My treat," he said.

"Can those earth tremors be felt underground?" Talbot asked as they clumped down the boardwalk toward Burke's Saloon.

"Oh, yeah. And down there, you can't just run outside to avoid something falling on your head . . . like a few million tons of mountain."

Burke's Saloon was full and the two men finally found a table only large enough for two tucked into a corner by the front window.

"I generally drink whiskey, neat," Granger said, "but this place has the best lager in town."

They discussed the weather and the earthquakes and the great prison breakout until well into their third beer. "I been working mostly labor jobs since we last saw each other," Granger said. "Some of my work choices haven't been the best . . . the railroad job got stopped by Indian attacks, then that scout with Forsyth that didn't end good. More recently, I mined for a few months, and quit when I damned near got caught in that Yellow Jacket fire a couple weeks ago, then this prison guard thing and you know how that ended. . . ." He shook his head and took a long draft of his beer. "So fill me in on what you been up to."

Talbot brought him up to date on his itinerant printing jobs.

"Well, at least you got a trade, and now been promoted to reporter, too. Except for knowing how to set a dynamite charge to blast out ore, I don't have any skills that're in demand. I'm thirty-one years old. Time I get into something permanent." He leaned back in his chair and crossed his legs. "I reckon you know I want to ask you why you left that night on the island," he said, loud enough to be heard above the cacophony of voices and laughter, the whirring of a roulette wheel, and the clinking of glassware.

The alcohol was relaxing Talbot. If he couldn't confide in Phil Granger, the least judgmental of men, there was no hope for the rest of the human race. "You want to know the truth?"

Granger nodded. "Been wondering about

it for a long time. Figured you must've had a good reason."

"I figured there was no hope, and I had a lot of living left to do."

"I can understand that. I was scared myself."

"It wasn't like getting married 'until death do us part.' I didn't feel obligated. We were just out of options, and I decided it was time to move on. When the colonel asked for volunteers to go for help that first night, I should have stepped forward."

"The newspapers were wrong about one thing."

"What's that?"

"They called you a coward. No such thing. They were quoting Sergeant McCall."

"McCall's concept of military honor means nothing to me. Giving up my life would not have saved even one of my comrades."

"You're absolutely right. I wish you'd asked me to go with you."

"Time to put that battle behind us. You ready for another sip from the River Lethe?" He held up his empty glass for a refill.

"Don't tell me!" Granger said. "Lethe . . . the river of forgetfulness. From Dante?"

"Correct. Wouldn't it be nice if there were a river like that . . . where memory loss could be selective?"

"You inspired me to educate myself, to read the classics," Granger said. "And I've become a better man for it."

One of several roving waiters arrived with two fresh, foaming mugs. Granger tilted his and took several long swallows.

A scuffle broke out across the room and Talbot heard shouts above the din. Then the boom of a shotgun filled the space. Men scattered, some reaching for their guns as they rushed toward the front door, others diving to the floor.

Talbot jumped to his feet, knocking his chair over backward. He caught a glimpse through the thinning crowd of a man holding a short coach gun, powder smoke drifting upward through the light of the chandelier. A bartender leaped over the bar with a shotgun in hand. The shooter swung around and let go the other barrel with a deafening roar. The bartender's white apron exploded in a spray of red as he went down.

A big man tackled the gunman from behind, and Talbot's view was blocked. The rest of the crowd rushed in to pin the shooter to the floor.

CHAPTER FOURTEEN

Talbot shoved forward to get a closer look, but he and Granger were both carried out the batwing doors on an ebbing human tide. A minute later, from the street, they saw a half dozen cursing men hustle the shooter past, dragging him toward the jail at the end of the block. The sagging man's face was bloody.

"Get a doctor!" a voice yelled from inside the saloon.

"No need. They're both dead," another replied.

The moon etched black shadows in the street as the crowd began to break up and drift away. It was just another shooting few wanted to witness or be near. The papers detailed such things every day — an unpleasant fact of life on the Washoe.

Talbot's reportorial instincts surged. "I'll get the details for a story," he said to Granger, and forced his way back inside. He elbowed to the spot where the two bodies lay within a few feet of each other. The shotgun had made a bloody mess, and Talbot glanced quickly away. "I'm with *The Gold Hill Morning News,*" he said to no one in particular. "Saw the shooting. Anybody tell me what caused it?" He had his pencil and notebook out.

"They's both drinking. This 'un was winning and the other pulled out a coach gun and let go. Then he shot Sam when he come over the bar to stop it."

"That's the way it happened, all right." Several others nodded agreement. "Sam Rice was the best man in this town when it come to helpin' men down on their luck. Ran a tight place here, but a squarer man I never saw."

A bystander stripped off his coat and spread it over the dead bartender's face and chest.

"Did somebody go after the coroner and the sheriff?"

"Yeah."

"Anybody know the name of the shooter and this other dead man?" Talbot asked.

The men crouching near the bodies looked at each other and shook their heads. "Don't know this 'un. The gunner was a sport around town who played piano here and there in saloons. Name's Al Heffernan. Has a hair-trigger . . . especially after a few drinks. Got into a few scrapes and keeps getting fired."

"Thanks, boys." Talbot closed his notebook and slid out of the crowd back into the fresh outdoor air where Granger was lounging near a hitching rail.

"The shooting was over a card game. They were drunk."

"Figured as much," Granger said as they crossed the street, dodging a passing buggy.

"Sam Rice, the bartender, was mighty well liked, apparently. Man named Al Heffernan was the shooter. Wouldn't want to be in his shoes, judging from the mood of that crowd." Talbot suddenly felt sober and tired. "I need to get some sleep."

"You gonna hoof it over the divide to Gold Hill? The omnibus quit running hours ago."

"No matter. It's only two miles."

"A lot of men afoot get held up going that way at night," Granger said. "You're welcome to bunk in my room, if you don't mind the hard floor. I got an extra blanket."

"Thanks, but I should be getting back. I want to be at the paper when Doten shows up. He has his hands full with two papers, and he'll need help." He glanced at the three-quarter moon. It had to be at least

2:00 in the morning. "Now that you're unemployed again, you can sleep later." He laughed. "See you tomorrow."

Next morning, when Talbot reached the pressroom, the extra edition of the paper was coming off the press. He'd overslept, but it didn't matter. Alf Doten was at the door, shuffling the thin edition into stacks and handing them to eager newsboys to hawk on the streets. Talbot grabbed a copy and glanced at the front page. *PRISON BREAK* was a banner head, *by Special Correspondent Matthew Talbot.* Just below that was a smaller head: *Inside Details of Massive Escape From Carson City Prison.* Then in still smaller lettering, the last bold-type teaser: *Fifty-four men rampage, kill six guards, and wound others, including Lt. Governor. No escapees recaptured.*

Talbot scanned the columns of smaller type and saw his piece had been printed as written. Doten had trusted him to write and set it, electing not to change a word. All the editor had done was write the leads. The inside of the four-page paper was filled with later national news from the telegraph wire.

"Good job on that story," Doten greeted him, looking up. He was puffy-eyed from lack of sleep. "I had fifteen hundred copies run off. We should sell most of them. You got the details. Don't know how you did it or who your unnamed source was, and I don't care to know. I heard the prison officials clamped down on letting out any news. You sure you didn't just create some of these details?"

"I had a source I trust, but I can't give his name."

"That's all I need to know." He handed the last stack to a boy who trotted away, yelling: "Extra! Read all about the big prison break!"

"If you want to stay on for a time, I'll increase your pay to forty dollars a week," Doten said. "You can help edit the paper as long as I have to fill in for Dan DeQuille at *The Territorial Enterprise.*"

"There's a lot more to editing than writing articles," Talbot said.

"I'll show you how to do layout and cut," Doten said. "I'll select which pieces go where and write the leads."

"Fine. I'll do it." Talbot nodded, wondering if he was being drawn into more responsibility than he was ready to assume. He mentally set a three-month deadline for trying out this new job. He could save enough to quit and move on to another job. Granger would have found a job by then and possibly moved on as well.

"I wrote up the details of a double killing at the International Saloon last night," Talbot said. "In case you might want it for tomorrow's paper."

"Damned right I do."

"A friend and I witnessed it from across the room. Sam Rice was killed."

"Oh, no! One of the best men I ever knew."

"That's the general opinion."

"Write it and set it in type. Leave it on my desk." He turned away. "I have to hitch a ride over to Virginia and collect a couple of advertising fees, then work on *The Enterprise*. Be back later today," he added. "A lady friend and I will be attending the theater tonight." Apparently no amount of work interfered with his social life. "Do you ever go to plays?" he inquired.

"Actually I went last night with a fellow I know. That earthquake ended the performance early."

Doten chuckled. "You'll get used to that. Happens pretty regular around here. Between those and the underground blasting, the earth is dancing a jig most of the time. That's one reason I like this area . . . something going on day and night, either man-made or Nature reminding us she's here. You ever hear of a Washoe Zephyr?"

"Yeah. How will I recognize one from a regular wind?"

"Well . . . when one end of a log chain is hooked to a post and the loose end blows straight out from the post, that's a normal wind. When the links begin to snap off, that's a Washoe Zephyr."

"Surprised there's a building left standing."

"Frankly so am I. If we ever have a big fire when a Zephyr is blowing, one of two things will happen . . . the wind will blow out the flames, or the whole damned town will burn down and the embers scatter into the eastern Nevada desert."

"What show you taking in tonight?" Talbot asked.

"*Court and Stage* with Miss Evans as Nell Gwyne. That's at the Tivoli. But there're lots of different shows to choose from. *Lady Audley's Secret* at the Opera House, a variety show at one of the others."

"You like the theater, I take it."

"I try to hit 'em all. My lady friend loves to go out, too. If a man can't find something to interest him among all the variety shows, socials, and traveling dramatic troupes, he's a mighty dull fella."

"I'm meeting a friend in Virginia this evening. We might check out one of the theaters." He was beginning to enjoy himself. Virginia City and Gold Hill attracted many of the best shows and amenities of the larger cities. Why not stay here for a time? He might even consider putting down roots here. Plenty of excitement and distractions — a boomtown that never got dull.

He and Doten walked down the street and had a sandwich for lunch. Talbot drank two beers to file off the rusty edge from a late night.

Doten was more or less a continuous drinker who seldom showed any signs of his imbibing. Talbot knew that he himself didn't have the physical stamina to be a drunk. It would take a stronger man than he to drink to excess every day or night and still be able to function. The agonies of being sick and hung over every day would be more than he could stand. Although, from what he'd seen, there were degrees of drunkenness, he didn't want to make a study of the problem. Dan DeQuille, well-liked editor of *The Territorial Enterprise,* was such a man who managed to keep his job the majority of the time. The paper's owner, Mr. Goodman, knew and forgave the foibles of his best editor, and hired him back after every spree.

From what Talbot had observed, the consumption of spirits and beer probably kept Gold Hill, Silver City, and Virginia City running, just as surely as any amount of gold and silver mined here. Gambling, drinking, and whoring were the main attractions for mostly single men whose lives would have been unalleviated drudgery without these wilder distractions to soak up their excess cash.

That afternoon Doten instructed him on how to prepare the next morning's edition. Then the editor wrote a few leads, reworded some articles, proofed some pieces set in type, included two travel letters from friends at Yosemite, inserted two pieces of light verse, then left to catch the omnibus to Virginia City to perform DeQuille's job.

Later that night, Granger and Talbot opted to see the play, *Mary, Queen of Scots*. Talbot was surprised at the quality of the performance. "Can't believe how good the actors are," he remarked to Granger when they left the theater. "Guess I just figured as isolated as we are from big cities, all performances would be second-rate."

"An oasis in the wilderness," Granger said. "This is like a little San Francisco dropped into these desert mountains. Whatever money can buy, will be found here . . . from oysters and champagne, to Cuban cigars and New York's first-run plays. The millionaire mine owners see to that. Actually there's so much money circulating that nothing is out of reach."

"I suppose you're right. It must cost a fortune to buy and transport these massive Cornish pumps and the other mining machinery from the factories around the Horn to San Francisco, and have them hauled by wagon or rail over the mountains to be installed here."

"Takes millions to pay for that," Granger agreed. "So you can imagine how much high-grade ore is being dug out of the Ophir, the Consolidated Virginia, the Gould and Curry, the Mexican, the Potosi, the Yellow Jacket, and all the other mines along these mountains." He shook his head. "I can't stretch my imagination around all of it. And I did my share to blast and shovel a good bit of that ore during the past months."

The two men were strolling down the sidewalk toward the International for a drink, when Talbot spotted Alf Doten with a buxom woman on his arm.

"Mister Doten!"

"By God . . . Talbot! I've never seen you so dressed up."

"Been to the theater."

"This is Matilda Metz," Doten said, presenting the woman, who nodded and extended a gloved hand.

"This is Matthew Talbot, who works for me."

"Phil Granger, an old friend of Matt's," Granger introduced himself.

"You headed somewhere in particular?" Doten asked, suddenly serious.

"To have a drink."

"Can it wait a bit? That fella Heffernan who shot those two at the International last night is in jail. Sheriff sent word to me by messenger not ten minutes ago that the prisoner wants to tell his story to the paper. I'm tied up just now." He glanced fondly at Matilda. "If you could interview him, I'd be obliged. If it's something worth printing, you'll get a by-line."

"Sure. I'll go see him. Guess if he wants to tell his story to the world through the newspaper, he won't mind if I take a witness along to verify that I got his words right." He glanced at Granger. "Mind?"

"Hell, no. It might be interesting . . . although I'd think a murder suspect would want to wait till his trial to present his case."

Doten chuckled. "A man can often get public opinion on his side if he publishes his own version of events first."

"Reckon so," Talbot said doubtfully. "But that might not be enough. A lawyer will have a tough time defending this Heffernan. A whole roomful of people saw him shoot two men."

"Extenuating circumstances." Granger shrugged. "But every man should have his day in court."

The door was locked when they reached the sheriff's office attached to the jail. A light shone in the barred window. Talbot knocked.

"Yeah?"

"Matt Talbot from *The Gold Hill Morning News.* Came to interview your prisoner."

"Which prisoner?"

"Albert Heffernan."

"One minute."

They heard movement and a key grated in the lock. The door swung inward.

"He's back here." The jailer locked the door and took up an oil lamp and led the way into a hallway that had barred cells on both sides. He paused and unlocked the first door he came to. "Can't go in there with your guns. Leave 'em with me." He disarmed the two, put the guns on the desk, and then pulled a short, fat candle from his pocket and lit it from the lamp. "He don't have no fire in there, even to smoke. You'll need this to see." He handed Talbot the candle and locked the cell door behind them. Talbot dripped wax onto the tiny wooden table in the cell and stuck the candle upright.

The prisoner stood up from his bunk. "Thank God you came," he said. "You from the paper?"

They introduced themselves without shaking hands. Heffernan was a slim man of average height with curly black hair and a haunted, hollow-eyed look that bespoke of much sleeplessness. Talbot was surprised at how young he appeared.

"This couldn't wait until morning?"

"Time doesn't have any meaning in here."

Granger sat down on the board bunk that had a thin blanket thrown over it.

Heffernan paced the eight-by-ten-foot cell, rubbing his hands. He had long, tapered fingers.

"I wanted to tell my story to Sheriff Atkinson, but he wouldn't listen. Said to save it for my trial. Guess he's used to all his prisoners proclaiming their innocence. But that's not what I'm doing. I want to trade what I know for my life." He put a hand to his swollen, split lip.

"So why don't you save it for your trial?"

" 'Cause the mob that dragged me here's in no mood to wait for a trial. I'm afraid something is going to happen to me soon, and I want to be heard quick. If the sheriff won't listen, I'll tell the whole world and then maybe, if or when I get to trial, my attorney will plea bargain me a prison sentence in place of the gallows."

"Go on." Talbot turned so he'd catch the candlelight on his notepad.

"The man I shot was Bill Card . . . one of the escaped prisoners from Carson. Don't know anything much about him, except he paid me fifty dollars up front and promised another fifty if I'd let him lay low in my room until the heat was off and he could slip out of town. But he wanted a drink. Shaved his head, glued on a fake mustache, put on some old clothes, and we went to the saloon. *Ah,* what a mistake. We got t'playing poker and drinking, and the drunker we got, the more I lost, and the more he gloated as he raked in the pots. I'm not really a poker player, so I couldn't tell if he was cheating, or just having one helluva streak of luck." He paused in his pacing and looked directly at Talbot. "Well, you don't need to know every little detail. To cut this a bit short, the last hand he won was like a spark to a fuse. It cleaned me out. I grabbed the coach gun I'd brought along for protection and just blew that damn' grin right off his face." His eyes blazed in the wavering candle flame. "Then the bartender came at me with a scatter-gun and I just reacted before I thought. Reckon if I hadn't been so drunk, none o' that would have happened." His voice sank in utter despair and he put his hands to his face.

"Is that all you've got to say?"

"No."

"You think a lynch mob will come for you because you shot the bartender?"

"Yeah. But I got an ace in the hole that will save me from the hangman if I can get me a lawyer and live to go to trial."

"What's that?"

"I know where all that gold is stashed that disappeared from the mint back in late winter."

Talbot looked at Granger who was leaning forward, staring intently at the prisoner.

"Yeah, Jake McCall and I stole that gold two months ago, and hid it."

"That name's familiar," Talbot said. "Was he a former Army sergeant?"

"Yeah."

"Was he at the Beecher Island battle?"

"That's right. You know him?"

" 'Fraid so. But go on. . . ."

"Well, McCall was working security at the mint, captain of the watch. Not a very likable fella, and didn't have many friends hereabouts 'cause he got mean when he drank . . . and he liked his liquor. I played piano in a lot of saloons and we got acquainted. Anyhow, after we got to be friends, he took me into his confidence, mainly because he needed a man to help him relieve the mint of a lot of misstruck gold coins that were stored in the vault. I agreed to help him since I was hurting for money most of the time, trying to get by on what tips I made playing piano. I was able to round up several empty dynamite boxes for him. They were small and stout, just what he needed to load all those little tubes of double eagles. He picked an April night when one o' those Washoe Zephyrs was blowing to beat hell. Dust so thick you couldn't see more'n fifty yards. He had me drive his wagon behind the mint, and we used a dolly to load those dynamite boxes of gold coins, and nobody the wiser." He paused in his pacing and shook his head. "Amazing how easy an inside job can be when it's pulled off by a man who has a position of trust. We covered the load with a tarp, drove off, and hid it in a safe place. I left the wagon at his place, and he rode his horse back to the mint in time to end his shift. On a night like that, nobody was looking for him. Said he got the idea of using the weather as cover when a blizzard was raging the night he discovered the gold in February."

"Where'd you hide it?"

"That's what I can't tell you. I'm saving that piece of information to bargain for my life."

"So you and McCall are the only ones who know?"

"That's right. McCall and I planned to haul that three hundred pounds of gold coin out of Nevada, but we had to wait till the spring mud dried up and the roads were passable."

"The gold was never missed?"

"Oh, yeah. Norman Whitley, the mint director, raised hell about it. Auditors were sent to the mint but found everything in order and accounted for. No record of any misstrikes. Whitley had to publicly admit he was holding the misstruck coins, but was planning to melt them down to make new ones. He was severely reprimanded by the Treasury Department for not doing it immediately after the coins were minted. A lot of suspicion fell on Whitley, but he stuck to his story and didn't resign."

Talbot glanced at Granger, who nodded. "There was a lot of stuff about it in the papers before you came to town."

"Is this Whitley a tall, white-haired, elegant-looking gent?" Talbot inquired, probing his memory.

"Yeah. He was appointed director sometime last year."

"That must have been the man who helped me on the stagecoach," Talbot murmured. "Reckon there's a little larceny in 'most everyone."

"Who?" Granger asked.

"Tell you later," Talbot said, turning back to the prisoner. "Where's Jake McCall now?"

Heffernan shrugged. "Wish I knew. He quit his job. I haven't seen him in two weeks. God, I could've been in luxury for the rest of my life . . . if I'd stayed sober," he lamented, touching his split lip. It'd begun to ooze again. "I'd never have to play piano in saloons again."

"Aren't you afraid McCall will hear about you being here and try to cart off the gold without sharing?" Talbot asked. "If you can't have any of it yourself, maybe it's better you make public the hiding place so McCall can't make off with it. The court might still be lenient if you come clean now and we print the information."

Heffernan paused, frowning, the soft candlelight on his battered face. "McCall might have already taken it and left town. If I tell you the location, but it's already gone, what then?"

"You could hardly be worse off than you are now," Talbot said.

The wall clock in the front office chimed 1:00.

"This will be in tomorrow's paper," Talbot said, stuffing pencil and pad into his shirt pocket. He turned to call for the jailer, when there was a loud pounding on the front door.

The jailer came to his feet. "Wait a minute!"

But with a sudden screeching of nails pulling out of wood, the door crashed inward, splintering the frame. A man burst in, holding a pry bar, followed by two others, all hooded and holding rifles. The jailer staggered back and four more men entered.

"Gimme the cell keys!" a voice demanded from behind one of the masks.

"Who the hell are you?" the jailer yelled. "Get out of here!"

"Vigilantes!" Heffernan gasped, cringing back into the shadows.

Talbot reached for his .32 in the small

holster at his belt before he realized he'd given it up to the jailer. Granger looked equally frustrated when he grabbed for his weapon that wasn't there. Talbot snuffed the candle.

There were sounds of a scuffle. The jailer was forced off to a side of the room by two hooded Vigilantes wearing long dusters. Another at the desk declared: "Here're the keys!"

Now the men trooped toward the jail cells.

"Ho! The killer's got company!" one of the vigilantes cried. He held the lamp high and peered into the cell. "Stand aside, gents. We got business with the prisoner, and don't want no interference."

Talbot and Granger looked their helplessness at each other while they backed away from the cell door.

A key grated in the lock and the door opened out; several men crowded inside. "Heffernan, we've come to hang you for two murders."

"Without a trial?" the accused cried.

"No need for that. At least sixty witnesses saw you do it."

"I was drunk. Didn't mean to do it. It was an accident."

One of the men guffawed at this.

"I'm entitled to a trial! It's the law," Heffernan whined, his face ashen in the lamp-light.

"A waste of time and money," one of the men said. "Too many miscarriages of justice at the courts down in Carson City to take a chance."

"Get your boots on. You're coming with us."

Heffernan slumped down and made a weak effort to pull on his boots. "My feet are swole. I can't get 'em on."

"No matter. You can swing in your sock feet."

"Let me have a last word with my lawyer then," he said, leaning over to say something to Talbot.

"What for? A lawyer won't do you any good where you're going."

"I was just giving him a message for my poor old mother," the prisoner said. "Just a couple of seconds. . . ." He put his mouth close to Talbot's ear and whispered: "We hid the gold in an old mine shaft. A thousand feet west of the Geiger Grade. Up Cedar Hill Ravine in a collapsed mine tunnel."

"Enough!" Big, raw-boned hands jerked the prisoner away from Talbot. "Your mother knows she raised a good boy." An oily laugh coiled out from under the hood.

A chill went up Talbot's back. That voice, that laugh. "McCall!" he gasped. The two holes in the flour sack turned to regard him. "Who the hell you talking to?"

Rough hands yanked the slim piano player out into the hall and pushed him toward the rear door.

"Jake McCall! Is that you?" Heffernan cried. "I didn't mean to kill nobody. I was drunk and mad. The bartender just surprised me and my gun went off, that's all."

"What about these two?" someone shouted, pointing a rifle at Talbot and Granger.

"Bring 'em along. We can't afford to have anyone running off to get help. Lock up the jailer in a back cell. Our Vigilance Committee is not going to be accused of kidnapping a lawman."

"Splittin' hairs, if you ask me," another man grumbled.

"Nobody asked you."

It was apparent McCall was in charge.

"McCall, you ain't got no business in the Vigilantes. You're a damned thief!" Heffernan yelled. "You and I stole the gol—"

A fist to the jaw snapped Heffernan's head back. He slumped, unconscious, between two big men who dragged him toward the door.

A man jammed a chair against the broken front door and followed the rest out the back into the alleyway. It was then Talbot saw the patrolling mob of hooded men swarming to join them from the street in front and back. The phalanx of men, bristling with rifles to keep the curious crowd from following, marched along A Street to Sutton Avenue. They climbed a low hill to the Ophir Mine where a small building stood over one of the oblique shafts. From the front of this building, a beam projected twelve feet above ground level. Beneath this beam, a set of rails led out to the end of a short trestle, allowing ore cars to be run out and dumped into waiting wagons below.

A man laid a board across the track on the trestle, and Heffernan, hands bound behind him, was forced to stand on it. Someone hurled a coil of rope over the upper beam and adjusted the noose around the neck of the condemned man.

Four vigilantes gripped the arms of Granger and Talbot, standing eight feet away.

"This man deserves a fair trial!" Talbot yelled, frustrated.

The back of a gloved hand stung his face, snapping his head sideways. "No talking."

The leader behind the flour sack stepped up to Heffernan, who stood rigidly silent, awaiting his fate. The vigilante leaned forward and whispered something to the condemned man.

"McCall, you'll pay for this!" Heffernan's face was ashen in the torchlight. "You'll pay!"

McCall stepped back.

"What's all the confab about?" a whiskey voice growled.

"Merely asked if he had any last words."

A booted foot kicked the loose board from under Heffernan who fell straight down, jerking up short at the end of the rope.

Talbot cringed at the agonized choking sounds, while the man desperately kicked and twisted. He slowly strangled, his face turning dark, eyes and tongue protruding. After long, agonizing seconds, he ceased to struggle. His body hung limply, swaying to and fro in the lantern light.

"You God-damned murderers!" Talbot shouted.

He saw the rifle butt coming too late. Spangles of light exploded in his head, and he fell into a dark hole.

CHAPTER FIFTEEN

"Matt! Matt!"

Talbot heard his name called, but couldn't respond. He must be dreaming.

"Matt, can you hear me?"

Someone was wiping his face. He made a concerted effort to speak, but heard only a croak issue from his mouth. Opening his eyes, he saw dim yellow light. He had to blink several times before his vision cleared. Rolling over, he started to rise when a sharp pain above his eyes halted him. He drew a long, shuddering breath, and fully regained consciousness.

Granger was staring at him with a worried look. "God, I thought your head was busted."

"Not so sure it isn't." Talbot gingerly felt his forehead. His fingertips came away bloody. "Those vigilantes play rough. Where's the one who hit me?"

"Long gone with the rest of that sneakin'

bunch," Granger said through his teeth, as he put an arm down and helped Talbot to his feet.

A lantern left burning on the ground nearby gave a soft yellow glow to the grisly scene of the body still dangling from the projecting beam.

"Thought maybe I dreamed all that," Talbot said, drawing his eyes away from the sight of Heffernan.

" 'Fraid not. Can you walk?"

"Yeah. A little dizzy, though. Lemme lean on you. How long was I out anyway?"

"Maybe five minutes."

"We'd best get back to the sheriff's office."

"That bunch o' bystanders probably already let the jailer out."

"I'm sure he knows what happened. We just have to tell him where to find the body."

They tottered down the hill and back into town, looking like two drunks.

"Crude justice," Granger said.

"It was more than justice," Talbot replied, as details of the lynching began filtering back into his memory. "I'm sure the leader was ex-Sergeant Jake McCall, that Beecher Island bastard. I'd know his voice anywhere."

"If what Heffernan told us is true, I

251

wouldn't be surprised if McCall didn't stir up the vigilantes to lynch Heffernan just to shut him up about the location of the gold," Granger said.

"Heffernan had a hunch it was coming, or he wouldn't have asked to see a reporter late at night," Talbot said. He stumbled in a rut and gasped as fresh pain shot through his head.

When they reached the jail, Sheriff Atkinson and the jailer were standing out front talking to a group of about fifteen men who'd apparently liberated the jailer. The sheriff was wearing his pants, gun belt, and hat, but only a long underwear top. "Ah, here they are," the jailer said. "A bit the worse for wear," he added as Talbot came into the light from the open office door. "Give us the bad news."

Talbot filled in the details of the hanging.

"Damn!" the sheriff swore with feeling. "The murderin' bastard deserved to hang, but they should've let the law handle it. If this keeps up, the county will have my job for sure. Those vigilantes can hide behind masks and get away with anything. I admit they've scared off a bunch o' no-goods, but they never know when enough is enough. Were you able to identify any of that mob that did it?"

"No," Talbot lied. He was making no accusations on the basis of his memory of a voice from the past.

"By the way, you fellas left your guns on the table in the office," Atkinson said. He turned toward the door. "Lemme put on a shirt while a couple of you men hitch up a wagon and we'll go bring the body in." As if he'd had a sudden thought, the sheriff whirled and jabbed a finger at Talbot and Granger. "You two leave me your names and addresses. You'll be witnesses at the inquest."

After retrieving their guns and giving the location of where the hanging had occurred, the pair moved away. Granger pulled out his watch and read the big face by moonlight. "Nearly half after two."

"I'm in no shape to write that story tonight," Talbot said. "I'll bunk at your place till daylight. Have to be back at the paper by eight."

"You can have the bed."

At 11:30 that morning, Talbot scanned the proof sheet of his lynching story due to go into the next edition of *The Gold Hill Morning News*, reading parts of it aloud as Granger and Doten listened. ". . . about three o'clock in the morning, Sheriff Atkinson

253

and Deputy Higbee found the body suspended where the vigilantes left it. Only his hands were tied. Pinned to the left lapel of his coat was a small placard on which was written . . . 'Al Heffernan . . . committee number six-oh-one.' " He ran a finger up under the white cotton bandage snugged around his wounded head.

"The coroner was summoned and brought the body in a coffin to Wilson and Brown's undertaking establishment on B Street where hundreds came to view it, as Heffernan had been a popular piano player. The body was afterward taken away by some women to a house farther south on B Street. There, with the assistance of some male friends of the deceased, it was properly washed and prepared for burial, then removed to Keyes undertaking establishment on C Street.

"Coroner Symons held an immediate inquest in the matter. Dr. Green testified that on examination of the body he found the neck not broken, therefore the deceased must have died from strangulation. Messrs. Talbot and Granger, who were interviewing the prisoner at the time he was forcefully removed from the jail, testified the masked men kidnapped them and took them along to witness the hanging at the Ophir Mine.

"The verdict of the coroner's jury was to the effect that the deceased was aged forty years and that he came to his death on the Fourteenth day of June, Eighteen Seventy from strangulation by hands unknown, in the city of Virginia, Storey County, Nevada." Talbot lowered the paper. "You want to hear about funeral plans?"

"No!" they said in unison.

"You know, it's not too late to publish Heffernan's tale," Talbot said. "This states the dry facts, but people really want to read the story behind the story."

"We can't publicly accuse Jake McCall of a crime without proof. Heffernan, the only witness, is dead," Doten said.

"We wouldn't be accusing him," Talbot countered. "We'd only be reporting what Heffernan told us. And Granger is my witness to what he said."

Granger nodded. "That's right. Men who are about to die have no reason to lie."

"No, I don't feel right about it," Doten demurred. Stubble showed on his cheeks above the goatee. He yawned and stretched. "Missus M wore me out last night." He got to his feet and opened his office door to admit a stirring of outside air along with the clatter and voices from the adjacent pressroom. He turned back to them. "If we

255

publish anything about this, I want it to be the final chapter of the story. Otherwise, we'll have people searching for gold coins in every empty mine shaft on the Washoe."

"From what I heard Heffernan say, it shouldn't be hard to find."

"Hell, we can't be dawdling around," Granger said, getting up and pacing to the door. "McCall could be there right now, loading it into a wagon."

"He didn't have time last night. And he wouldn't chance hauling it off in daylight, especially if it's been hidden there since the theft two months ago. McCall has gone to a lot of trouble, so he'd be careful now to make sure he got it. His partner's dead, so he thinks nobody else knows the coins are in Cedar Ravine," Talbot said.

"That's right," Doten agreed.

"OK, to settle this, let's go get those gold coins . . . if they're actually there . . . before anyone else has a chance to," Granger proposed.

"I have a date to take Missus M to a variety show tonight," the editor said.

"Is that more important than this?" Talbot slowly grinned, looking from Granger back to Doten, who was absently flipping the metal cap on his desk-mounted inkstand.

"Hell, you want to run your fingers

through those double eagles as bad as we do," Granger urged.

"Even if we find it, we can't keep it," Doten said. "Those misstruck coins have to be returned to the mint." He didn't sound totally convinced.

"Even if mint director Norman Whitley planned to steal them, and his former captain of the watch, Jack McCall, *did* steal them?" Talbot objected, nervously touching the bandage on his head.

"The way I look at it, those coins are salvage," Granger said. "If Heffernan described them correctly, he helped McCall remove them from the vault, but they no longer belong to anyone because the official records show those coins were disbursed. They're not on federal property. They have no one's name on them. They're anyone's to claim . . . like pieces-of-eight from a sunken Spanish galleon."

"We're not talking about the laws of salvage that apply on the high seas," Doten said.

"Are you an attorney?"

"No."

"Then it's finders keepers," Granger said.

The three men were silent for a minute. Talbot thought the others were likely contemplating what they could do with about a third share of all that money — $31,000 each at face value.

"Let me have a word with you." Doten motioned Talbot toward the outside door. "Excuse us a minute," he said to Granger. "Nothing against your friend, but I just don't know him that well," he explained outside in the glaring sunshine. "I'm not sure why you brought me into this. . . ."

"Because you're my boss, and sent me to interview Heffernan," Talbot broke in. "You have a right to know. Besides, I respect you. You and Granger are the only friends I have around here. He and I go 'way back. If you hadn't made me a local reporter and sent me down to Carson to cover that prison break, I wouldn't have reconnected with him."

Doten stared off at the wagon and foot traffic passing up and down the main street of Gold Hill. "I don't reckon it's any problem of yours," he said slowly, "but I'm in debt up to my receding hairline. I owe the bank several thousand for a loan to buy this paper, and I'm still trying to pay for that new steam press. My ongoing overhead here with several employees is considerable." He rubbed a hand over his mustache and goatee. "As far as income is concerned . . . well, it's dropped off some because of competition for sales of advertising space and job printing for such things as handbills, ballots, tickets. . . ." His voice trailed off and he turned to look squarely at Talbot. "*Ah,* hell . . . the truth of the matter is I have a compulsion to speculate in mining stock. And I've taken a beating lately."

Talbot waited, wondering where all this was leading.

"If it weren't for me losing money, I wouldn't think of going after that pot at the end of the rainbow you described. But I'm desperate, and willing to take a chance that what Heffernan told you is true."

Talbot felt a grin capturing his face. "Welcome aboard." He followed Doten back into the office.

"I'll rent a wagon and a team of mules," Doten said to Talbot and Granger. "Don't know what we'll run into, so we gotta be prepared for anything." He picked up several proof sheets from his desk. "I have a paper to run the rest of the day, but you round up a pick axe, a fifty foot coil of stout rope, a shovel, and two lanterns. I'll bring a canvas cover in the wagon." He paused, looking at both men. "Not a good idea for all of us to be seen together, so you two meet me on the Geiger Grade just north of the Union Mine at half past seven. You know where that is?"

Both men nodded.

"Good. I'll need the last hour of the daylight to drive the team up that steep, winding trail into Cedar Ravine. Don't bring any horses, and try not to attract unnecessary attention. Can you lug that stuff on foot?"

"Yeah. One tow sack should do it," Talbot said.

"I've been on the Washoe a lot longer than either of you," Doten said, loosening his .44 Colt conversion revolver in its holster, "and I have butterflies about this. Be sure you come armed."

CHAPTER SIXTEEN

"You brought *what?*"

"Half a case of dynamite sticks, some blasting caps, and a coil of fuse," Granger said, lifting a bundle of red, cylindrical sticks out of the wooden box on the floor and wrapping the fuse around them. He slid them carefully into a heavy cotton sack on the bed. A small box of blasting caps followed.

"What're we going to blow up?" Talbot raised his eyebrows, nodding at the ominous bulge in the sack.

"Never know what we'll find out there. Heffernan and McCall could have buried that stuff or set off a charge and covered it with a couple tons of loose rock," Granger replied. "You don't think they left the stuff just lying in plain sight, do you? A pick and shovel may not be enough." He gestured at the tools in a second cotton sack. "Here's a coil of new, stiff rope, two lanterns full of coal oil, and a block of lucifers."

Talbot nodded, swallowing a lump in his throat.

"Let's get at it," Granger said, shouldering the sack of explosives. "We got a ways to hike." He moved toward the door of his room, then looked back. "Don't worry. This stuff is safe to tote around. Nitroglycerine is what's not stable. The heat will make the nitro sweat out through the paper on these sticks, then it could get a bit chancy. But I've handled enough of this in the mines to know what I'm doing. I'll keep it in the shade and fairly cool."

"Familiarity breeds contempt," Talbot said. "What about the blasting caps? Every week some kid around here blows off a couple of fingers messing with those. They find 'em lying around the mines on the ground and start playing with them."

Granger chuckled. "Trust me. I treat blasting caps with respect, like I treat a loaded gun."

Talbot shouldered the bag of tools and rope, his stomach tensing. "Let's go." He rested his palm on the ivory grip of the .32 Smith & Wesson snugged into a small holster on his belt. The pistol was not designed for long-range shooting. Talbot carried it for self-defense. Its four-inch barrel made it accurate up to fifty feet or so, and the weapon was light and comfortable to carry, so he wasn't tempted to leave it behind wherever he went.

Granger, when fired from his prison guard's job, had walked off in uniform, carrying the Smith & Wesson .44 top-break revolver he'd been issued. "Makes up for the last week's wages I didn't collect," he had growled when Talbot had questioned him about returning it. Both men carried extra cartridges.

They clumped down the outside stairway of the rooming house and started north along the shadowed street where swampers in the saloons were already lighting their lamps and propping doors open for the night trade and to catch the cooler evening air.

Talbot had the uneasy feeling all eyes were on them, everyone on the street wondering where they were going. Yet, he knew it was only his imagination. They blended into the crowd as well as any two miners could blend into a mining town.

On the hillsides above town, the buildings housing the hoisting works of various mines glowed in the setting sun. Talbot couldn't identify each of the adjacent mines they passed, but knew they had to go beyond the

Union Mine and just this side of the Sierra Nevada before they met Doten with his wagon and team on the Geiger Grade.

He trudged along the street, swinging both unlighted lanterns in one hand by their wire bails, the sack of tools slung over his shoulder. The pair drew hardly a glance. In their old clothes with the pick and shovel handles protruding from the sack, they could be mistaken for two men going to do assessment work on a small claim.

The buildings thinned out near the end of the dusty street. The sun was behind the mountains to their left. To their right was the building where Heffernan had been hanged less than twenty hours earlier. Atop the hill, the square, red building stood out in stark relief in the last rays of sun — the makeshift gallows of the jutting beam now empty. Rough justice or just plain murder for gain? Talbot wondered.

A quarter mile farther on, Granger stepped to one side to allow a freight wagon to pass, then averted his face from the dust churned up by its wheels. "There he is," he said, when the air cleared. He pointed at a lone figure on a wagon parked by the side of the road a hundred yards farther.

They reached Alf Doten and placed their sacks in the wagon bed. Granger stepped up on a wheel hub and settled himself in back, cradling the sack of dynamite.

"There's room up here," Doten said, patting the space on the seat between himself and Talbot.

"Thanks, but I'll tuck myself up next to my baby, to keep it from jostling." He grinned.

"What?" Doten said.

"Dynamite," Talbot explained.

Doten gathered the reins and pulled the heads of the mules away from the sparse grass they'd been nibbling. He popped the reins over their backs and started up the grade toward the mouth of Cedar Ravine. The wagon bumped along slowly in the gathering dusk.

"You've been up this way before?" Talbot asked.

"Yeah, but on foot. Took a look at a mine to invest in. Turned out to be a bust. No ore at all. Glad I kept my cash in my pocket when they began selling shares. Not always that lucky." He clucked to the mules as they slowed on an upgrade.

Fifty yards to their right, the rails of the Virginia & Truckee made a long curve into the Geiger Grade and headed off to the north toward Reno. A black locomotive and tender with several ore cars waited on a siding, just below the Sierra Nevada Mine. The engine had steam up and he could hear it panting softly. Likely waiting for the night shift to load the ore cars before it pulled out at daylight, and headed south to the stamp mills along the Carson River.

The wagon jolted into a rut.

"*Whoa!* Careful, there," Granger said quietly from the back of the wagon. "This stuff is pretty stable, but I don't want to put it to the test just yet."

"Doing the best I can," Doten said. "Getting dark. We should've started an hour ago." He paused. "Well, I doubt it would have made any difference the way this road is washed out."

The wagon squeaked and groaned over the rocky, rutted soil. The mules' iron shoes clicked and skidded on slabs of rock exposed by erosion.

"How far up this cañon did Heffernan say it was?" Granger asked.

"A thousand feet, as I recollect. But I was in no position to be taking notes at the time."

The tall, iron-rimmed wheels ground slowly along, thumping in and out of washouts. Talbot cringed when the wagon jolted into a deep hole, hoping the wooden spokes and axles were strong enough to withstand the punishment.

Doten eased back on the lines. "That's it. We'll have to walk the rest of the way." He wrapped the reins around the brake handle and stepped down. Talbot and Granger followed. Doten struck a match and lighted both lanterns, handing one to Talbot. The three men moved forward, single file, with Doten in the lead, Talbot next, and then Granger, bringing up the rear with the volatile explosives.

All vestiges of the abandoned road disappeared and they clattered and slid over rocks and gravel in the bottom of the gully. Cedar Ravine still retained a few stunted cedars that escaped the axe and the fierce winds from the summit of the mountains above.

Darkness wrapped itself around them, and the men walked, looking down into the bobbing circles of light of the lanterns to see where they were placing their feet.

They rounded a slight bend in the cañon and Doten stopped suddenly. "There's something up ahead."

Talbot looked away from the lantern light for several seconds to let his eyes become accustomed to the gloom. Sure enough, above and to the left was a rectangle of black against the face of the hill's lighter colored soil.

They stopped and Doten shuttered the lantern. Their deep breathing was the only sound in the stillness. "Let's go." He opened the lantern and they moved slowly, carefully up the steep slope, slipping and sliding in the loose detritus that had been cast down the hillside when the tunnel was dug.

The trio arrived at the mouth of the tunnel and Doten thrust the lantern inside. Twenty feet in, the mountain had begun to reclaim the vacated space. Tons of rock and earth had crushed the timbers down to the floor. Cobwebs festooned the sagging supports and the floor was sprinkled with pack rat droppings. Where the cave-in had occurred, a timber was wedged against the wall, holding back rocks from completely blocking the tunnel. It formed a triangular opening between floor and wall.

The men moved inside, treading softly as if to avoid breaking the spell of the place, or fearful the vibration of their voices might trigger another cave-in.

Talbot squatted and held his lantern to the opening that was barely three feet tall by three wide. It went back for at least a dozen feet. "Can't see the end of it. I'm the smallest. Let me try to crawl through." The others made no objection while he stripped off his jacket, and flattened out on his belly. Shoving the lantern ahead of him, he proceeded to wiggle his way into the opening. There was just enough space for a few inches clearance on each side and over his head. Three feet in he froze to allow a brown recluse spider to scamper away from the light near his bare hand.

The cave-in proved to be only about ten feet thick, front to back. He'd just started to feel claustrophobic when the lantern he was shoving ahead of him emerged into an open space. He followed it into the tunnel, stood upright, and brushed himself off. The support timbers were still intact and the light he held aloft dispersed into the darkness beyond. He had no idea how far the tunnel extended. But, as he looked around, he had a sinking feeling they were in the wrong place; there was no sign of the treasure they sought.

He went to his hands and knees. "I'm through to the other side of the cave-in!" he shouted through the opening. "The tunnel is still intact here! I'll explore farther!"

After a few seconds, he heard Doten's dim response. "Careful you don't trigger another cave in."

"Any sign of the boxes?" Granger added.

"No!" Talbot started back into the moun-

269

tain, wondering if there was any way to tell how close these beams were to letting go, allowing tons of earth to bury him. He should have sent Granger — the experienced miner — in first. But very seldom was the actual danger worse than the imagined danger.

Thirty feet farther, the tunnel took a slight downward cant. No ore car rails had been laid in here. Apparently this was an exploratory thrust into the mountainside in hopes of encountering a vein. The timbering suddenly ceased, and Talbot paused, uncertain how much farther he dared proceed. Rocks and dirt from overhead had sifted down in small piles here and there, the irresistible weight of the mountain pressing slowly downward. He stooped to avoid bumping his head on the lower ceiling. The tunnel grew smaller as if the miners had realized by this point that this was a lost cause as far as striking any promising ore, and were giving up the job. He stumbled over an abandoned pick with a broken handle.

Talbot looked back over his shoulder, but he was far enough down the tunnel that he could no longer see the cave-in where he'd entered. He became aware of the growing heat, and the fact that his breathing was slightly labored. The flame in the lantern was flickering lower from lack of oxygen. He prayed that no odorless gas had seeped in to fill the dead air space.

He was about to start back when his light glinted off a piece of metal. He thrust the lantern forward. It was a metal hasp on a box. He drew a deep breath. There it was — a stack of small wooden dynamite boxes near the wall. Each box was only two-thirds the size of a Wells, Fargo treasure box, and none was locked. The ten boxes Heffernan had told them about were all here. His heart began to beat faster. He set the lantern on the lid of a box and wiped his moist forehead. Lifting the topmost box by its rope handles, he set it on the floor and flipped open the lid. A jumble of sausage-shaped rolls lay in the bottom. He counted ten of them. He picked one out and used his clasp knife to slit the tightly wrapped muslin covering. Several double eagles trickled out into his palm, glowing softly in the warm yellow light. He looked at them closely. The coins appeared uncirculated, but the face of liberty was scarred the same way on several. They were indeed misstruck. The details of the hanged man's story were falling into place. By a rough calculation, the weight of all this, including boxes, was three hundred and fifty pounds. With the weight of three men and their tools, it all amounted to under a thousand pounds — an easy enough load for the wagon and mule team, without need for a heavy ore wagon.

He pocketed the coins to show the others, then replaced the tube in the box and closed the lid. His heart rate began to slow. It was, he reminded himself, only a little less than three hundred pounds of metal. It wasn't the end of the world. He stood up, stretching his cramped legs. Would they dare keep it? A question for later. The first thing was to move these boxes to a safe place.

He carried one box back up the tunnel to the cave-in. "I found it!" he yelled into the opening. "I'll start shoving them through, one by one."

Excited exclamations came from the other end. Without waiting for a reply, he headed back for the next box.

In thirty minutes, he had retrieved all ten of them, shoved them through the hole far enough to be grasped and pulled to the other end. He was perspiring and panting by the time he'd finished and crawled back through himself. Dirt coated his sweaty shirt and pants when he'd wiggled out and stood up, holding the lantern, gratefully breathing the fresher air.

"By God, it was true," Doten said quietly,

the three of them facing each other in the subdued light. "I wouldn't have given a silver ten-cent piece for the chances of that."

"I had a hunch Heffernan was playing straight with us," Granger said. "It ain't like a man to lie when he's under a death sentence." He held one of the gold coins up to his thick blond mustache. "What do you think? Is it a match for color?" He chuckled. "I reckon that means I was destined to keep it." His blue eyes were bright with excitement.

"I don't think you'll have to look for a job any time soon," Doten said. "In fact, I can get out of debt and finally make some money. Might even think about looking for a wife to settle down with."

"What're you going to do with yours, Matt?" Granger asked.

"Then we're agreed on keeping it? No thought of returning it to the mint where it came from?"

"None."

"Did you notice the misstrike?" He removed one of the coins from his pocket and held it out.

"It'll still spend."

Doten looked thoughtful. "Easy to trace, though. If we start spending these around here, we'll be in big trouble quick."

They were silent for a few moments.

"Well, we can discuss this later," Doten said. "Right now, let's haul these boxes down to the wagon. We can't take them to your rented rooms. I believe the safest place will be in my root cellar behind the newspaper office. Then we can decide what to do with them."

"I'll relieve you of that worry, boys."

A chill shot up Talbot's sweaty back as he whirled toward the familiar voice.

"Keep your hands in plain sight," the voice ordered. Thrusting a long-barreled Colt ahead of him, the big, raw-boned figure of ex-Sergeant Jake McCall moved into the lantern light.

CHAPTER SEVENTEEN

Hard-eyed Jake McCall, no longer wearing the authority of sergeant's stripes, eared back the hammer of his big Colt, alert to fire if any of the three moved.

Talbot's chill passed, leaving his heart pounding at this sudden apparition.

"So, it's the one who hightailed it from Beecher Island," the husky man said, eyeing Talbot. "You recognized me last night."

"Yeah."

"A very good recollection for voices after all this time."

"It was also your hands, your height, and the way you moved."

"*Ah* . . . a reporter with powers of observation." His eyes narrowed. "I should've been a mite quicker, and hauled my treasure outta here a week ago. But I didn't want Heffernan to go screaming to the law. No need to worry about him now."

Without taking his eyes from them, Mc-

Call flipped open the top of the nearest dynamite box atop the stack. Colt steady in one hand, he reached in with the other and pulled out a rolled tube of the coins. He hefted it, flicking his gaze to his hand, then back to the three men. "*Ah,* looks like I got here just in time to keep you from takin' my property." He placed the roll back in the box and dropped the lid.

"*Your* property?" Doten arched his eyebrows.

"I'm claiming surplus government property. That's all."

"These coins were misstruck at the U.S. mint where you worked. How do you figure government gold is your property?"

McCall grinned widely, his bent nose even more prominent. "I suppose you boys were up here in the dead of night just so you could return these coins to the mint and ask for a reward?" He barked a harsh laugh.

McCall stepped to the tunnel entrance and glanced outside. "Enough of this conversation. Time to go. But first. . . ." He paused and looked carefully around. "You there, coward . . . I forget your name . . . take your coil of rope and tie Mister Doten to that support timber against the wall."

"The name is Matt Talbot." He moved reluctantly to do as ordered.

"Mister Doten, turn your back to the post. That's it. Now . . . hands behind on each side of the timber. Now you've got it. Tie him, coward."

Talbot made the loops and knots as loose as possible without being obvious.

"You'd best make them good and snug," McCall said, standing back, revolver still steady on Granger. "I'll check the job when you're done. If it's not tight enough, I'll shoot your ear-lobes off." He chuckled. "Damn, that'd be a funny sight, now, wouldn't it? A coward with no ear-lobes. Well, I reckon the Indians would've done a lot worse."

"Any shots would be heard," Talbot said.

"Yeah, I guess I'd scare the jack rabbits." McCall snorted. "Who the hell is going to hear shots, as far as we are from town? Especially since we're inside a mountain."

Talbot secured the knots, but tried to avoid cutting off circulation in Doten's wrists.

"Now, slice off the rest of that rope and tie my other Beecher Island scout to that opposite timber."

Staring at the big black muzzle, Talbot obeyed.

Ten minutes later, Granger stood immobile, his back to the upright support on the opposite side of the tunnel. McCall directed the remaining rope be used to tie one man's ankles to the other's ankles, across the five feet of the tunnel width.

McCall then stepped forward and ran his hand over the knots, checking the tightness of the bindings.

Granger's shoulder muscles bunched under his shirt as he lunged against his restraints. The timber ground a few inches out of alignment, showering down dirt and rocks from the ceiling.

The overhead support was partially splintered and sagging.

"I'd be careful of struggling and jerking at those ropes if I were you," McCall said. "Or you could bring down this whole place on your heads." He smiled with obvious satisfaction. "Now, then, coward, hand me that clasp knife. Then throw those handguns back inside the hole under the cave-in."

Talbot complied.

"There are six leather bags with a coil of rope on two mules outside," McCall said. "Load them up with the rolls of coins from those boxes, so that each bag is about the same weight. Then, tie four bags across the wooden pack saddle, and two across my riding saddle on the other."

Talbot hesitated, looking at his two companions. He sized up McCall out of the corner of his eye, probing for a moment of inattention, a spot of weakness. He found none. Apparently McCall knew what he was doing.

"Oh, make no mistake about it, coward . . . *uh,* Tolbert, or whatever you call yourself, I'll cut you down with a bullet if you make a move to bolt or to come at me."

Under McCall's watchful eyes and the barrel of the loaded revolver, Talbot toiled for the next forty minutes to release the hobbled mules, lead them up close to the tunnel, and transfer the tubes of coins from the dynamite boxes to the leather bags. He was breathing heavily and sweating long before he finished.

"Well, that saved me a good bit of work," McCall said, moving into the light from just outside the tunnel entrance where he'd been carefully supervising. "I'd take you with me to unload my mules at the train, but that'd be too chancy trying to keep an eye on you the whole time." He looked around thoughtfully. "In spite of what you called me last night, I'm not a murderer. Too bad my code of honor won't allow me to just cave in that tunnel on the three of you and be done with it." His gaze fastened on the gash on Talbot's head where he'd removed the bandage.

"One of the boys took offense at your loud mouth," he said. "I thought maybe he'd done you in. But you evidently have a thick skull."

Talbot felt his pulse throbbing in the wound and carefully touched it with his fingertips.

"Don't worry, I won't slug you again. *Hmmm. . . .*" He picked up a six-foot piece of cord left from tying the leather bags across the backs of the mules. "Come with me." He forced Talbot out of the tunnel at gunpoint and they trudged up the ravine another fifty yards. "This'll do. Lie down on your belly."

McCall tied his prisoner's hands behind him. Then, bending Talbot's knees, he bound wrists to ankles and looped the last of the rope around his neck in a slipknot.

"There." McCall stepped back. "The classic hog-tie. If you start thrashing around, trying to get loose, you'll tighten the slipknot and choke yourself."

"You're really like strangling people, don't you?"

McCall made no comment.

In the dark, Talbot could vaguely see McCall moving away down the ravine. "I won't gag you," the older man said over his shoulder. "Nobody could hear your yell up

280

here. Maybe somebody will find you by tomorrow, but I'll be long gone by then. On the other hand, maybe they'll find your bodies next month. Life is a gamble."

A low laugh drifted back to Talbot, and then all he could hear was the clicking of stones as the man scrambled back to his loaded mules.

CHAPTER EIGHTEEN

Talbot lay hog-tied, listening to McCall making his way down- slope in the darkness. Twisting to one side, he saw the yellow square of light marking the tunnel entrance about fifty yards away. McCall's blocky frame appeared in the light. The muffled sound of voices, and then the lantern was snuffed out. Granger shouted something that sounded like a curse.

The shout faded, followed by the sound of boots scuffing on loose rocks. The raucous braying of a mule broke the stillness. Anyone within a half mile would have heard the noise. But a west wind was blowing, and they were around a bend in the ravine; the road was a long way below them. He strained his hearing, barely able to detect the clicking of iron horseshoes on rock growing fainter as they receded down the ravine. Then, silence.

McCall and his loaded mules were out of

earshot. Because of the load of coins and the uncertain footing for the animals, McCall was probably leading the mules toward the main road that ran north and south along the Geiger Grade.

Talbot strained to free his hands. He couldn't just lie here and let the man get away. But every time he moved his hands or his bent legs, the hemp collar tightened a little more around his neck; panic rose in his gut. He swore under his breath. McCall had effectively put him out of action. Rocks were digging into his chest and stomach. He rolled over slightly — and gasped at a sharp prick in his side. Sudden moonlight revealed a patch of low-growing cactus pads. He wiggled a few inches away. Rolling carefully onto his side, he could see high clouds scudding across the face of the gibbous moon, alternating light and deep shadow.

There had to be some means of escape. The rope he'd used to tie Doten and Granger had been new, oiled hemp he'd bought himself, and was much stronger than the old, worn rope McCall had used to hog-tie him. He lay still, thinking, conserving his strength, fighting down the panic of a choking sensation from the slipknotted loop pressing against his windpipe. His muscles were already beginning to cramp from the unnatural bowed position of his body. He'd have to think of something quickly.

Slowly and carefully he inched onto his back until his bent legs and bound hands rested on the ground behind him. Something jabbed his left ring finger. He sucked in a breath. His first thought was that he'd rolled onto a snake and been struck, but his probing fingers encountered the jagged edges of a broken bottle. He could feel sticky blood between his fingers.

Sweating, gasping, the rope pulling against his throat, he managed to position the bottom of the bottle flat on the ground, the jagged edges pointing upward. Working by feel, he moved his bound wrists into position and began sawing at the pieces of rope between them. One slip and he could cut an artery in his wrist and bleed to death.

Every minute or so he had to stop and rest, relaxing his straining muscles. Then he took a deep breath and started again, working patiently, carefully, until he felt the fibers of the rope begin to part. He continued to saw until the loop was finally severed. Moving his hands a few inches from the base of the broken bottle, he twisted his raw wrists until he began to feel the bonds loosening. Once his hands were freed, he quickly untied the slipknot from his neck, and, bending his fingernails and cursing, he wasted precious minutes picking at the tight knots on his ankles; his clasp knife had been left in the tunnel. He swayed to his feet, rubbing the circulation back into his arms and legs and staggered down the rough terrain toward the mine tunnel. Intermittent moonlight allowed him to find the entrance.

"Change your mind and decide to finish us off?" Granger snarled.

"It's me," Talbot panted. "Where're the matches?"

"Matt! There's a block of lucifers in that tool sack somewhere around your feet."

"Where you been?" Doten's voice came out of the dark.

"Hog-tied up the hill a ways."

Talbot fumbled with the block of matches, pulled off one, struck it on the stone floor, and relit the lantern. He recovered his clasp knife from the floor and began slashing at the bonds.

"You're bleeding," Granger said.

"Cut my hand on a broken bottle I was using to get loose."

"Here, I'll finish up," Granger said, taking the knife to release Doten. "You crawl into that little space and get our guns."

Talbot squirmed into the small opening

under the cave-in and retrieved the three pistols.

Granger flipped open the loading gate of his new Smith & Wesson and blew dust from around the cylinder. "Where'd he go?" he asked.

"Down the ravine toward the road in the grade," Talbot said, shoving his .32 into its holster. "From there, who knows?"

Doten stretched and swung his arms, glancing toward the tunnel entrance. "You think he'll see this lantern light and come back?"

"No." Granger kicked one of the empty dynamite boxes that littered the floor. "He's sacked up the gold and gone."

"If he'd wanted to kill us, he'd have done it when he was here," Talbot agreed. "He said something about murder being against his moral code."

"More likely he knows murder is a hanging offense," Doten said, "where theft generally isn't."

"We got to stop him," Granger said.

"I'm not risking my life for government gold," Doten vowed. "As long as the stuff was lying here for the taking, I wasn't above collecting my share. But going after an armed and desperate man is another stick of type altogether."

"While we're gabbing, McCall and his loaded mules are making tracks," Granger said.

Talbot looked out into the sooty darkness. The moon was again obscured by clouds. "Let's go if we're going."

"See you back in town," Granger said to Doten.

"You taking one of these lanterns?" Doten asked.

"Nope. If he ain't already out of reach, he'd see us long before we got near him."

"What do you aim to do if you catch up with him?"

"Take the gold," Granger said, jamming his hat on.

"He won't give it up without a fight."

"He surprised us tonight, but he won't again," Granger said. He glanced around. "Just in case, I'm taking this." He scooped up the sack with the dynamite sticks, blasting caps, and fuse. He twisted the neck of the cloth sack and slung it over his shoulder. "We'll save your share," he said to Doten. He motioned to Talbot and they slid out into the night, moving slowly down the slope to give themselves time for their eyes to adjust to the dark.

"It sounded like he was leading the mules, instead of riding one," Talbot said.

287

"Then he can't move fast until he reaches the road."

"We can't, either."

Granger slipped on the loose shale and caught himself with one hand against the side of the steep grade.

"Careful with that dynamite."

"It'll take more than a few bumps to set it off."

Talbot had his doubts about that, but said nothing, straining to see where he was going. He was busy enough just avoiding clumps of cactus and shifting his weight when rocks rolled under his boots.

In the rush of the chase, adrenaline was pumping, and Talbot was distracted from thinking about himself, concentrating only on their quarry. He stepped into a rut and felt his leg start to buckle. He couldn't stop his momentum, but redirected it by instantly shifting weight from his leg as he tucked his shoulder and rolled, sliding to a stop in front of Granger who'd pulled up short.

"You all right?"

"Yeah, but gimme a second or two," Talbot gasped, checking himself for injuries. Even though he hadn't struck his head, last night's wound was throbbing. "Just scraped up a little." He got to his feet. "Let's go." He brushed himself off and made sure his gun was still in its holster. "How much of a head start you think he has?"

"No more than fifteen or twenty minutes, I'd guess," Granger said. "But I got to slow down. If I fall on a sharp rock with this sack, it won't matter how much of a start he has . . . you and I'll be spread all over the side of this ravine."

By silent consent, the two men took a quick breather, Talbot staring downhill, straining his eyes and ears for any sign of McCall and his laden mules.

The moon came out from behind a cloud and Talbot was startled by a movement less than thirty yards away. "Damn! I forgot we left this wagon and team."

"Shall we leave 'em for Doten?"

They silently considered their options.

"No," Granger finally said. "I'll put this dynamite in the wagon and drive back slowly to the road. Safer that way. You can make better time by going ahead on foot."

Talbot imagined a hot slug from McCall's gun tearing into his chest, stopping his heart. He took a deep breath to calm himself. McCall might not be a calculating murderer, but Talbot was certain the man, desperate as he was to get away with his gold coins, wouldn't hesitate to kill. He swallowed hard and began to reassess the way they were pursuing their quarry. "Good," he heard himself responding to Granger. "Take the wagon and team. I'll go on ahead." He tried to keep the reluctance out of his voice.

They reached the wagon and Granger stowed his sack in the back, then climbed to the driver's seat and unwrapped the reins from the brake handle. He pulled the animals' heads around and clucked to them. They threw their weight into the harness and drew the wagon up out of a sandy rut.

Talbot stepped back and watched to be sure Granger didn't need his help to get the rig turned around in the narrow, washed-out remains of the road. Then he moved on ahead, trying to recall how far they had come up the ravine. He estimated he was about two hundred yards from the road below, and jogged ahead by the light of the moon. Then flying clouds blotted the luminescence, and he stopped to listen. He heard nothing but his own harsh breathing and the thumping of his heart in his ears. That, and the wind sighing softly in the stunted shrubs. Did McCall anticipate being followed so soon? He could be waiting in ambush up ahead to gun down any pursuers. Anyone finding their bodies later wouldn't know who'd killed them or why, until Doten told his story. *But that won't help if I'm dead,* Talbot thought. *Life is all about surviving . . . to at least three score and ten. It isn't about taking reckless chances and dying young.*

While these thoughts flashed through his mind, his eyes and ears stayed alert to any sound or movement ahead of him. But the ravine was as quiet as a tomb.

He reached the road in the Geiger Grade without seeing or hearing anyone. The rail siding for loading ore from the Union Mine was somewhere nearby. Looking up and down the road, he pondered which way McCall might have gone. It made no sense for him to turn right and go back to Virginia City and Gold Hill. Anyone trying to escape would be more likely to turn left, away from town and go north in the direction of Reno where miles of desert and mountains provided many places to hide the gold again, if necessary. The coins weighed about three hundred pounds. If McCall wanted to ride one of the mules, he could have transferred all but one of the bags to a single animal to distribute the weight evenly without over-burdening either. Each mule would then be carrying about two hundred and fifty pounds, and would be reluctant to move faster than a walk. In his experience, mules were smarter than horses and knew their limits, whether it was eating or packing loads.

Several minutes later, Granger pulled up in the wagon. "Any sign of him?"

"No."

"Reckon he got clean away?"

"Couldn't have gone too far yet. He's likely on this road somewhere, but I don't know which way."

"We could unhitch these mules and ride bareback. You go one way, I'll go the other," Granger suggested.

"Hell, I couldn't stay atop a trotting mule without a saddle," Talbot said.

"Know what you mean. Best we go in the wagon."

Talbot climbed up onto the left side of the seat. "Let's head for town. We can alert the sheriff in Virginia City to wire Reno to watch for him. He might strike out cross-country, but then lack of water would be a problem for him."

"Reckon that shoots our chances of getting our hands on any of that gold," Granger said, sounding depressed.

"Doubtful we could've kept it, anyway," Talbot said. "Likely just wishful thinking." He was almost relieved the decision had been taken out of their hands.

"Hyah!" Granger snapped the lines over the backs of the team.

They'd gone less than thirty yards when a hissing blast of released steam sounded somewhere ahead, followed by the heavy, rhythmic chuffing of a locomotive beginning to accelerate.

"That's the locomotive we saw parked on the siding by the Union Mine hoisting works," Granger said.

"Yeah, with steam up, ready to haul a load of ore to the mill," Talbot said. "Somebody's working mighty late."

"Sometimes they haul ore at night," Granger said.

"Don't you remember McCall saying something about taking me along to load the sacks on a train?"

Granger shook his head. "Guess I wasn't listening close."

"My bet is he's on that train with the gold and heading south."

"He couldn't get those mules aboard. That engine had only ore cars coupled to it."

"He didn't take the mules, just the bags."

The moon was popping in and out of the scudding clouds, and Talbot saw the black bulk of a mogul engine moving, less than fifty yards ahead.

"It's pulling out of that siding and headed

south toward Virginia City," Granger said.

"Far past Virginia City and Gold Hill, I'd bet," Talbot said. He leaped off the wagon. "Go for the sheriff. I'm going after McCall."

"What if he's not on the train?" Granger yelled after him.

"Then we haven't lost anything but a little time." But Talbot, sprinting away, was as certain of his hunch as he'd ever been of anything.

He was too late to isolate the train on the siding by throwing the switch. No switchman was in sight, so this was no scheduled ore run. He doubled his efforts, feet flying, arms pumping as he ran. The last ore car cleared the siding and the train was on the main line, gathering speed.

Talbot now found himself unable to gain on the slow-moving train. Too much beer, too little exercise. It was showing. He was out of condition. "Rats!"

The locomotive was not the common 4-4-0 American. It was a 2-6-0 Mogul freight locomotive, with its smaller drive wheels, designed for power rather than speed. And it was pulling five ore cars.

Talbot gave it everything he had. Within three feet of the last car, he made a lunge and managed to snag the iron ladder just as the car was pulling away. He was twisted sideways, his arm nearly yanked from its socket. He hung on while his boots scuffed gravel. He reached desperately and got his other hand on the iron rod. Then it was a matter of muscling his body up by sheer strength until he could get his feet under him on the bottom rung. There he hunkered, gasping, until he recovered enough to climb up and over the lip of the deep car. It was empty. From his higher perch, he looked forward and saw by moonlight the other four cars were also empty. Just as he guessed — this was no ore train. Who would he find in the cab? If McCall didn't know how to operate one of these machines, it was likely he'd commandeered both the engine and its crew.

Sliding down into the dirty car, he was appalled at how fast his physical strength had faded during his all-out sprint for the train. He crouched in the bottom of the car, legs trembling from exertion. He was sure no one knew he was aboard, so he gave himself a few extra minutes to slow his breathing and gather his composure. He had two things on his side — surprise, and the loaded .32 Smith & Wesson on his belt. In the event it came to a physical contest, he wasn't too sure he'd win. McCall was at least ten years older, and a drinker. But he was big, and looked to be fit. Desperation also figured into it. McCall had plotted and schemed to get his hands on these many thousands of dollars in gold, and wasn't about to let go of them now.

Talbot caught his breath and was regaining energy. If the fifty-pound leather bags were in one of these ore cars, maybe he could find and throw them off without being seen. He looked forward. Four cars ahead, the woodpile atop the tender was high enough to block a view from the locomotive cab.

The train was rocking along at forty to fifty miles per hour — faster than any ore train would have rolled through the heart of town.

Moving carefully, and gripping the edges of the swaying cars, he worked his way forward, climbing over the ends, stepping over the jerking, banging couplings to scale the rim of the next car. He was thankful this train wasn't hauling the customary thirty to forty cars. In the bottom of each ore car was the residue of dirt and gravel from its last load. He found no leather sacks of coins.

By the time he slithered over the back rim into the first car behind the tender, he knew the sacks must be in the cab or tender, or possibly tied underneath on the wheel trucks. But, from where he crouched, the tender appeared to be overflowing with chunks of firewood. If three men and two big seats occupied the cab, there probably wasn't room left for six leather bags.

Then two thoughts struck him, one after another. What if Granger was right, and this train had nothing to do with the fleeing robber? After he yanked a gun on the crew, could he just say he was sorry, it'd all been a mistake, and then jump off? Not in the dark, and not at the speed this train was going. The other consideration was more of an instinct than a thought. If he was right, and McCall and the gold were in the cab, could he subdue him? The ex-sergeant, as captor of the train crew, would certainly have his gun in hand, making it difficult to get the drop on him. McCall was sure to put up a fight. Talbot gripped the edge of the ore car. His survival instinct was rising. This fight he could not — would not — lose.

The squeal of air brakes shivered his eardrums. Inexplicably the train began to slow. Buildings of Virginia City were sliding past. Were they stopping at the depot? Why? His mind was in a whirl. The train slowed even more until it was rolling no faster than a man could walk. But it didn't stop. Talbot guessed the engineer, to avoid arousing suspicion, was barely creeping through town.

Peering over the rim of the ore car, he could see pedestrians and wagons on the main street some distance away. A sudden movement caught his eye and lights from open saloon doors flashed on a horse and rider galloping south along the street at full speed. The man sat a horse like Granger! But it couldn't be. No mules or wagon. Where the hell was he going? And where was the sheriff? *I must be seeing things.* The horseman thundered on ahead of the train and Talbot slid back into the ore car, rubbing his stinging eyes.

Smoke boiling from the balloon stack was whipping away on a west wind. Only now and then did a vagrant breeze and the train's forward motion fan a burst of wood smoke down, enveloping him in a choking cloud for several seconds. Eyes closed, he held his breath, feeling a layer of fine ash coating his face and hands. The spark arrester in the top of the bulbous stack kept live embers from flying out and setting anything afire.

Stalling the moment when he'd have to climb over the tender and down into the locomotive cab, Talbot drew his .32 and tested the action of the hammer and cylinder. Then he eased the hammer down, and re-holstered the weapon to free both hands for climbing.

The huffing, clanging, and rattling of the train would mask any sounds he'd make. He had to be careful not to fall. He eased over the forward lip of the empty ore car and let himself down, straddling the coupling. Steadying himself with one hand on the ore car and the other on the tender's ladder, he shifted and swung himself across and began to climb. As his head cleared the top of the woodpile, the wind snatched off his hat and whirled it away. The wood was not stacked; it was tossed into a jumbled pile, short sticks jutting up every which way, making it difficult to crawl across the top of the swaying car. He heard the iron door of the firebox slide open and then clang shut several times as someone was busy feeding fuel into the voracious maw beneath the boiler.

Talbot lay as flat as possible. Chunks of wood jabbed his stomach and chest. He drew his revolver and thumbed back the hammer. Pushing to his hands and knees, he started forward. He could just see over the pile. The stoker was leaning forward to toss a chunk of wood into the open firebox.

The orange light of the furnace glowed inside the cab. A man, pistol in hand, sat sideways in the engineer's chair, his beaked profile visible. He turned his head slightly and firelight fell fully on the face of Jake McCall.

CHAPTER NINETEEN

The fireman swung around for more wood and came face to face with Talbot. Eyes went wide in the round, soot-streaked face, and his mouth opencd in a startled yell.

Talbot leaped off the pile and knocked the man off balance.

McCall swung down the barrel of his Colt. Talbot dived behind the fireman as flame flashed from the muzzle. The fireman doubled over, clawing at his mid-section. He slumped sideways off the platform into the darkness.

Talbot fired, but the locomotive lurched and his bullet clanged off the face of the iron boiler.

McCall flinched at the near miss, but thumbed back the hammer of his big Colt. Scrambling out of the seat, his foot slipped and his revolver went off. The bullet ricocheted off the iron deck, stinging Talbot's left forearm. With no room to move, Talbot sprang at the taller man, slashing at his face with the gun barrel. McCall leaned back, avoiding the blow as Talbot cocked and fired again. His bullet punched a hole in the leather seat where McCall had been. Talbot crouched. McCall's next bullet shattered the water level gauge above his head, spattering them with water and broken glass. Talbot lunged upward, slamming his shoulder into the big man's mid-section and McCall's thumb slipped off the Colt's hammer. The weapon exploded beside Talbot's head, deafening his left ear. Talbot drove with his legs, forcing the off-balance man into a big, horizontal handle, shoving it forward. The engine abruptly slowed.

Grabbing McCall's wrist, Talbot shoved it upward. The Colt blasted into the roof.

Talbot's own gun hand was pinned under McCall's elbow. Locked together, both men staggered back and forth, straining for advantage.

McCall jerked his knee up sharply into Talbot's groin, breaking his grip. With a sickening rush of pain, Talbot fell backward, but was able to cock his pistol and blindly fire.

"You bastard!" McCall clapped a hand to his left ear. Blood ran between his fingers.

Talbot realized he'd jerked the trigger,

pulling the barrel off target. Nauseous from the pain in his groin, he couldn't follow up his advantage, and bent sideways against the opposite seat.

As the train slowed, McCall sprang to the throttle handle. Yanking it back, he released more steam into the cylinders. The locomotive responded and, with powerful strokes, began to accelerate once more.

Talbot raised his head, recovering just enough to point his Smith & Wesson. McCall turned and brought up his Colt. The engine lurched into a curve as both pistols roared. The shots went wild.

Ignoring his pain, Talbot leaped up, catching McCall's chin with his shoulder, snapping the man's head back. For a second McCall seemed stunned. Talbot swung his pistol like a club. But the blow lost its force as the top-heavy locomotive rocked upright out of the curve, and the two men clinched again.

Gasping, they stumbled into the sharp levers and handles. Talbot was vaguely aware of being struck in a dozen places. He ignored the pain, desperately focusing on one thing — keeping his opponent's gun from getting a clear shot at him.

Talbot sensed the man weakening as the struggle began to take its toll. He tripped

McCall, throwing him down against the hot firebox door. With a bellow of pain, he jerked away, the back of his jacket smoking. Talbot jammed a knee down on the wrist of the gun hand, pinning it to the deck. He reached down and twisted the Colt away, flinging it overboard.

"Now!" He jumped back, leveling his .32 at the man on the floor. "Get up in that seat."

McCall slowly rose as ordered, glaring his hatred.

Like some huge beast, the throbbing locomotive carried them along faster and faster. Talbot looked at the unmarked levers. He didn't know how to stop it.

The tall man dabbed at his bleeding ear with a bandanna, and appeared to be eyeing him for a chance to spring.

"Slow this thing down!"

"You're in control. You do it."

Talbot's chest was heaving as he struggled to catch his breath. Sweat trickled down his face. Holding his gun steady, he glanced at the circular steam pressure gauge. The needle crept back a notch. No one was feeding the firebox. He guessed it would take several miles for them to lose enough pressure to stop. They were going far too fast to negotiate safely two wide curves that lay ahead, just this side of the Crown Point Trestle.

Maybe he had time to get what he wanted. "Where're those coins?"

"What coins?" Though bested, McCall was still arrogant.

"They're hidden on this train or you wouldn't be aboard."

"If I don't kill you, I'll have you arrested for assault and attempted murder," McCall snarled.

"It won't be *attempted* murder if you don't tell me where those bags are, and then stop this train."

An oily laugh curled above the pounding of the locomotive.

Suddenly a blue-white glare lit up the cab with wavering light. Lightning? Keeping his pistol on his captive, Talbot thrust his head out the window. A brilliant phosphorescent glow lit up the sky. Trailing white smoke, it reached the top of its arc and started downward a half mile ahead. The artificial sun brightened the landscape, and revealed the approaching stretch of Crown Point Trestle.

McCall glanced out the right side window. "A warning!" he shouted above the noise, his defiant look gone. "There's a red flare on the tracks." He reached up and shoved

305

the big throttle lever forward. The train began to slow.

Talbot swallowed hard, glancing ahead. Shining silver in the phosphorescent light, the twin strips of steel bent into a long, sweeping curve. Would the engine slow enough to keep from derailing? The cacophony gradually diminished in volume, although the rattle of the empty ore cars, banging of couplings, and the pounding of the big push rods still made hearing difficult.

Now Talbot knew which one was the throttle, but still didn't know how to apply the brakes. The big, bellowing engine was running away with them. He'd seen many trains pulling everything from passenger cars to freight cars to ore cars go over the Crown Point Trestle, but none of them had exceeded fifteen miles an hour while crossing. The huge trestle, bridging the divide between Virginia City and Gold Hill, was one of the wonders of the West. People came from everywhere to view it and ride across it. From a distance, it appeared thin and spidery, a network of intricately placed sticks. But on closer examination, the structure was built of massive timbers bolted together and rising some hundred and fifty feet above the bottom of the gorge.

A slow ride across its narrow top with no railings on either side had been known to throw women into a fit of the vapors and cause strong men to hold their breath or ask for a stiff drink to steady their nerves.

In the dying light of the flare, McCall's face had paled.

The mogul locomotive was slowing, but not fast enough.

"Apply the brakes!" Talbot ordered.

McCall grinned. "The coward of Beecher Island showing the white feather at last?"

Talbot shoved the four-inch barrel of his pistol under the big man's chin. "Stop this train, I said!"

"Or what? You'll kill me? Not a chance. Apparently there's something up ahead that'll derail this train." He guffawed. "Or, one of your friends is trying to fool us into stopping."

It was the first time Talbot had considered this possibility. He'd seen Granger race ahead of the train more than two miles back when they were barely moving through Virginia City. Maybe Granger had set off the flares to trick them into stopping.

Talbot had only a few seconds to decide what to do.

McCall apparently read his face. His defiant attitude returned. "If there's real danger ahead, we'll face it together. After all, I don't have anything to lose. I might not hang for robbery, but I'll sure hang for shooting that stoker. Which of us has the most to lose?"

Once more Talbot leaned out the window. He could now see the red glow of a warning flare on the track a hundred yards ahead, growing more distinct as they rushed toward it. Into the long curve they went, Talbot bracing himself against the centrifugal pull. Steel wheel flanges squealed against naked steel rails while the locomotive fought like a live thing to stay upright.

"We're getting off this train." He grabbed McCall by the arm and yanked him out of the seat.

"We're going too fast."

"Then stop us."

"No."

"You want to die?"

"Do you?" That sinister grin again.

Talbot reached for the throttle lever and pulled it back as far as it would go. There was some way to throw the steam engine into reverse, but he had no time to figure it out. "I'm jumping." He glanced at the ground rushing past. They'd slowed, but he guessed they were still traveling over thirty miles an hour.

"Believe I'll take my chances and stay

aboard," McCall said with bravado. "I've cut the telegraph wires in both directions. If this turns out to be a bluff by your friends, I'll be long gone with my baggage, while you're lying back there all busted up." He laughed aloud. "Seems fair enough to me. You prepared to die, coward?"

In a surge of anger, Talbot sprang at the man and cracked him across the face with the barrel of his pistol.

"Aagghh!" McCall grabbed his bloody nose. "You son-of-a-bitch!"

Talbot jammed the .32 into its holster, gripped the handle at the rear of the cab, and swung out onto the iron ladder. Cool wind rushed past his overheated face. The sage-covered embankment was barely visible in the moonlight. The red flare still glowed beside the track at the edge of the trestle, only forty yards ahead. He took a deep breath and leaped out and forward.

It seemed he fell forever before his feet struck the steeply sloped bank and he flexed his knees in an attempt to break his fall, covering his head and rolling over and over, absorbing the shock. He felt himself being pummeled by rocks, brush and cactus spines tearing at his clothes. Finally he slid to a stop and looked up at the last ore car passing above.

A quick assessment told him he was still intact, although bruised, cut, and generally battered. The train was accelerating again, chuffing clouds of smoke from its balloon stack. It rolled out onto Crown Point Trestle at more than twice the safe speed. And it continued to roll, faster — faster. Had someone been signaling the train to stop? Or was the red flare a phony danger signal? The locomotive and ore cars diminished in size as they chuffed and rattled away from him, picking up speed toward Gold Hill and somewhere beyond.

Talbot sat on the dirt bank and swore softly to himself. There went his quarry with six fifty-pound leather sacks of double eagles. He sighed, beginning to feel every one of his cuts and bruises. The law might eventually catch up with Jacob McCall, but no thanks to Matt Talbot.

Boom!

Thunder from the far end of the trestle. Timbers ahead of the speeding train erupted into the sky, silhouetted briefly by a red fireball.

Talbot caught his breath and stared in fascinated horror at sparks shooting from the wheels of the locomotive. A long screech of tortured metal came as McCall threw on the brakes and spun the wheels in reverse

— but too late. Seconds later, the black freight locomotive tipped slowly forward and disappeared from view, dragging the tender and five empty ore cars after it. With the prolonged roar of a thousand angry grizzlies, tons of fiery iron plunged down through the wooden structure, rending, grinding, and crashing into the bottom of the gorge far below. A final boom sent a cloud of white steam upward as the boiler exploded.

Talbot's ears rang with silence, sprinkled by small sounds of splintered wood and shards of metal raining down like hail from a man-made storm. A cloud of smoke drifted across the face of the moon.

Talbot's breath rushed from his lungs. "God Almighty!"

Chapter Twenty

Three days later

"Had to run off another two thousand copies of that *Extra* yesterday just to keep up with demand," Alf Doten said. "You two are the most famous men in Washoe." Leaning back in his swivel chair, the editor laced his fingers across his belly and propped his feet on the desk.

The sibilant hiss and soft rhythmic clanking of the steam press sounded quietly through the open door from the pressroom as the new edition of the *The Gold Hill Morning News* was being cranked out.

"The Virginia and Truckee will likely take me to court for destroying their property," Granger said, pacing to the window and staring out at the foot and wagon traffic on the street.

"I doubt it . . . even though *The Virginia* was one of their finest locomotives," Doten said. "They stand to gain more in publicity

312

than they'll lose in dollars. This story will be picked up by all the big city newspapers and make the V and T name synonymous with high Western adventure. It'll attract people from everywhere."

"Rail traffic has been shut down until they repair the trestle," Granger continued, "costing the mine owners, the mill owners, the merchants, not to mention the lost passenger and freight revenue for the railroad."

Doten was unfazed. "They already have workmen swarming over that trestle. It'll be up and running again in ten days. You only blew out the last section."

"That locomotive probably cost as much as the gold we saved," Granger moaned, playing devil's advocate.

"Doesn't matter," Talbot said. "The owners will consider it the price of doing business. How would it look if the railroad owners took a hero to court?" He stood and stretched. He was so sore, he could barely move. But he dared not remain still for long, either, or his muscles stiffened. The swelling in his scrotum was subsiding, but was still painful. "You're the real hero. You'll only have to work for the railroad fifty or sixty years to pay off the damage."

He and Doten laughed, but a frown creased Granger's brow. "I was only trying to stop the man the best way I knew. And, being a former miner, I know how to set a charge."

"One thing that's been bothering me," Talbot began, "is how you were so sure I wouldn't be on that train when you blew up the trestle."

Granger shrugged. "Easy. You got better sense than to ignore those signal flares. I knew you were aboard, but I had to take a gamble that McCall and the gold were there, too. You seemed so damned sure, I had to take your word for it. That being the case, I figured McCall would never part with the gold he'd gone to so much trouble to steal. If I'd guessed wrong and a regular train crew was actually aboard, they would've stopped when they saw the flares, and I wouldn't have lit the fuse."

"You knew I had enough sense to jump off?" Talbot was skeptical. "Even if you were dead certain of that, I still could've been killed. That damned thing was going more than thirty miles an hour."

"Not everything in life is certain. Have to take a chance sometimes."

"Why'd you choose the Crown Point Trestle instead of just blowing the tracks and derailing it?" Doten asked.

"Too many houses and stores along the

right of way," Granger said. "Could've run off the rails, down an embankment, and killed more people, or set the whole damned town afire. And Virginia City already has its share of fires without me causing more."

Doten nodded. "Makes sense."

"Besides, once the train slowed and I got ahead, I wanted to give Matt a chance to get off," Granger said. "The sheriff didn't believe my story, so I didn't waste time trying to convince him. I just left the wagon and team at his office, grabbed my sack, and jumped on the nearest saddled horse I saw. Hightailed it south. Horse gave out and I had to borrow two more along the way. Busted the lock off a trackside tool shack to get those flares. Wasn't till I found them that I set the charge." He looked at Talbot. "Damned good thing the train nearly stopped in town. And then the tracks make a big curve away to the east before they swing back in and bend south toward the trestle. Gave me just enough time."

"Yeah," Talbot said. "For a while there we slowed down because we knocked the throttle closed when we were fighting. Then steam pressure started to fall when nobody was stoking." He shook his head. "If I'd known what was coming, I'd have jumped off before we picked up speed."

"Once you had McCall under control, why didn't you yank the Johnson bar and put on the brakes?" Granger asked.

"The *what?*"

"The Johnson bar. It's a big lever that sticks up out of the deck. Has a squeeze grip handle to release its ratchet. With the throttle off, applying brake pressure with that bar might've stopped you."

"Damn! A lesson learned a little late. You should've been aboard that engine, not me."

Granger's somber expression finally relaxed into a smile. "I had other duties."

"Well, McCall got what he deserved . . . crushed and scalded," Doten said. "But enough was left to identify."

"Damned glad the coroner's jury met quick and ruled justifiable homicide after you vouched for our story," Granger said to Doten. "It helps to have a leading citizen back us up."

"Good thing those sacks weren't full of paper currency," Doten said. "Gold is indestructible. Just scorched the bags." He looked at Talbot. "You played your hunch, and it turned out right. The bags were evidently under the wood in the tender. Too bad the sheriff got to them before we did."

The three men were silent with their own thoughts for a few moments.

"You thinking what you could have done with a third of all those gold double eagles?" Talbot asked.

"You're reading my thoughts," Doten said. "I'd have pulled myself out of debt and had a surplus to play with. Could have married." He got up and closed the door between his office and the pressroom. "As far as I know, the three of us and McCall are the only ones who knew we were planning to take that gold for ourselves," he said in a low tone. "And it has to remain that way. Let people and the law speculate all they want, but nobody can prove we weren't going to turn those gold pieces back to the government." He looked at each of them. "Agreed?"

"Agreed," they chorused.

"I have a little memento for you," Talbot said.

They looked their silent curiosity at him.

"When I first found those boxes in the tunnel, I put a few coins in my pocket to bring out and show you. But then I realized the boxes would fit through that opening, one by one, so I could just go ahead and retrieve the whole stash. When Whitley showed up, I completely forgot I had the coins." He withdrew his hand from his pants pocket and held out an open palm with six double eagles. "Two for each of us."

"I'll be damned," Granger said, picking out a pair of the coins and gazing at them. He heaved a long sigh. "What might have been. . . ."

"There're likely a few more scattered in the bottom of that gorge," Talbot went on, "because Sheriff Atkinson said one of the leather bags split open when the cars hit bottom. Word spread quickly and about half the town swarmed down there to scour the ground for any the sheriff and his deputies might've missed."

"We still came out on top," Doten said. "One of the Nevada senators has introduced a bill to authorize a reward of a thousand dollars be paid to each of the three of us. He says it's sure to pass. That's not to be sneered at . . . especially considering how tight-fisted the government has been even funding the Carson City Mint. A man can do a lot with a thousand dollars."

"I suppose you're right," Talbot said.

"And if I'm not held responsible for all that property damage, I'll be satisfied," Granger said. He looked at Doten. "And we have you to thank for the way you wrote that story."

Doten shrugged. "I was there. I'm only telling the lightly varnished truth. We're all heroes, and I, for one, am going down to the International to celebrate with a few drinks and supper. Afterward, Missus M and I are taking in *King Lear* at the Tivoli."

"That part about the few drinks sounds good to me," Granger said. "Hell, it's past noon . . . not too early to celebrate. A toast to the future."

Talbot felt his old friend's eyes on him.

"Not just now," Talbot said reluctantly, almost tasting a good, fiery brandy hitting the back of his palate. "This might be a good time to start cutting back on my drinking." He could hardly believe he was hearing himself say that.

"Damn!" Granger looked at him in wonder at this refusal. "You really *are* changing."

"Out with the old, in with the new," Talbot mumbled, feeling embarrassment flushing his face. "But don't start the beatification process just yet. I've still got a powerful thirst." He glanced at Doten. "Come fall, I generally quit my job and head for my cabin on the edge of Death Valley. But you asked me earlier about staying on at the paper."

Doten nodded.

"If that offer still stands, I'll take it. Full-time, year-around employment might kill me, but I'll never die any younger."

"That'll be good for both you and me."

Doten smiled. "In any case, you should stay around for a few months to bask in the glory that we'll all share from this adventure."

"But first I need a week or two to go visit my mother in Saint Louis," Talbot said, thinking to tell her the details of what happened. He wanted her to know that he was a survivor — that he wasn't reckless and foolhardy, that he'd calculated the risk and decided to take it. He'd fled Beecher Island to save himself, and been branded a dishonorable coward by the man who'd turned out to be a thief and killer. He'd tell her he'd actually attempted to become a thief himself, but was now branded a selfless hero. Public opinion wasn't always omniscient.

AUTHOR'S NOTE

Through the combined efforts of several survivors of the battle, and members of nearby Grand Army of the Republic posts, an inscribed marble obelisk was placed on Beecher Island in 1905. Civil War veterans held an annual reunion there for many years. In 1935, a spring flood washed away the monument. A few pieces of the base that could be found were placed near the new historic marker constructed on higher ground.

This site, located on the Arikaree River about seventeen miles south of Wray, Colorado, was placed on the National Register of Historic Places in 1976. The island itself, which was only a brushy sandbar, has been washed away by flooding over the years. A diorama of the Beecher Island battle is housed in the museum at Wray. The park is open to the public year around. A two-day reunion commemorating the battle is held each September and is open to everyone.

Alfred Doten appears as himself in this novel. A native of New England, he sailed around Cape Horn to the California gold fields in 1849. He began keeping a journal as a young man when he set off on this adventure. He continued recording daily events until his death more than fifty years later. From the early 1860s until 1903, he worked as a newspaper editor in Gold Hill and Virginia City, Nevada, and experienced the boom times of the Washoe region. Many years later, these voluminous handwritten notebooks were edited by Walter Van Tilburg Clark (author of *The Oxbow Incident*) for publication by the University of Nevada Press. *The Journals of Alfred Doten 1849–1903* appeared in three thick volumes in 1973, and were the source from which I mined many details of daily life to enrich this story.

ABOUT THE AUTHOR

Tim Champlin, born John Michael Champlin in Fargo, North Dakota, was graduated from Middle Tennessee State University and earned a Master's degree from Peabody College in Nashville, Tennessee. Beginning his career as an author of the Western story with *Summer of the Sioux* in 1982, the American West represents for him "a huge, ever-changing block of space and time in which an individual had more freedom than the average person has today. For those brave, and sometimes desperate souls who ventured West looking for a better life, it must have been an exciting time to be alive." Champlin has achieved a notable stature in being able to capture that time in complex, often exciting, and historically accurate fictional narratives. He is the author of two series of Westerns novels, one concerned with Matt Tierney who comes of age in *Summer of the Sioux* and who begins his professional career as a reporter for the Chicago *Times-Herald* covering an expeditionary force venturing into the Big Horn country and the Yellowstone, and one with Jay McGraw, a callow youth who is plunged into outlawry at the beginning of *Colt Lightning.* There are six books in the Matt Tierney series and with *Deadly Season* a fifth featuring Jay McGraw. In *The Last Campaign,* Champlin provides a compelling narrative of Gerónimo's last days as a renegade leader. *Swift Thunder* is an exciting and compelling story of the Pony Express. *Wayfaring Strangers* is an extraordinary story of the California Gold Rush. In all of Champlain's stories there are always unconventional plot ingredients, striking historical details, vivid characterizations of the multitude of ethnic and cultural diversity found on the frontier, and narratives rich and original and surprising. His exuberant tapestries include lumber schooners sailing the West Coast, early-day wet-plate photography, daredevils who thrill crowds with gas balloons and the first parachutes, tong wars in San Francisco's Chinatown, Basque sheepherders, and the *Penitentes* of the Southwest, and are always highly entertaining.